BILLIONAIRE COWBOY'S HILL COUNTRY PROPOSAL

Billionaire Cowboys of True Love, Texas, Book Three

HOPE MOORE

Billionaire Cowboy's Hill Country Proposal

A second chance romance about a billionaire bull rider and the girl he left behind. Rumors and secrets can tear a relationship apart, but can the truth mend broken hearts or is it too late for love?

Bull riding champion Bret Tanner is home to help with a family charity event, but when Ellie Seton shows up asking for an interview, he has no plans to open up to the woman who broke his heart years ago.

Ellie is desperate for the interview and not thrilled about having to convince Bret to talk to her. He broke her heart when he chose bull riding and a tabloid worthy lifestyle over her. Now, she's an entertainment columnist and needs this interview or she'll lose her job. When her mother, the town florist, is injured, Ellie must step in to help fulfill the flower orders for the Tanner family's charity event.

Can Ellie use helping with the event to get the interview she needs? Or will working side by side with Bret be too much for her heart to bear?

CHAPTER ONE

Ellie Seton smoothed the pencil skirt of her black suit and stared at the doorway of Manny's Bar and Grill in her hometown of True Love, Texas. She was not glad to be home. She swallowed hard and took a deep breath to steady her nerves. It had been a long time since she had set foot inside this bar and grill. Almost eight years, actually. She had been home a few times but had not ventured out from her parents' home much. Especially here, a favorite hangout for locals.

The last time she was here, it was with Bret Tanner. She could still feel her heart pounding furiously because he'd told her he had something important he wanted to ask her. *Something important...* She'd been such a fool. They had been out of high school a year when they'd started dating and had dated for over a year when she had believed he was going to ask her to marry him.

They had dated for a year after she had given her heart to him. He dreamed of being a champion bull rider and had been seriously pursuing his dreams, which made dating hard at times. But he was amazing, and they'd managed. She believed in him and could see him competing and winning at the NFR, the National Finals Rodeo in Las Vegas, or the pro bull riding at the PBR National Finals. She knew to reach that level, it would take dedication and that he would be on the road constantly competing, gaining points, and securing a rank that would take him to the finals. But she had thought he loved her and they'd find a way to do it. It hadn't worked out that way.

Standing on the threshold of the bar and grill, she swallowed down the heartburn that rose in her throat. She hadn't wanted to come here today. He hadn't asked her to marry him all those years ago. Instead, he'd asked her to wait on him while he went on the road to make his dreams become a reality.

His responsibilities on the ranch kept him busy when he was home because they needed him. But toward the end of their first year of dating his family struck oil and they could afford to hire more ranch help. This freed him up to pursue his dreams. And that was what he needed to tell her that night. He hadn't asked her to come along with him; instead, he'd asked her to wait for him.

It had broken Ellie's heart, but she had tried to wait for him.

But when a cowboy is on the road—especially a wealthy, talented cowboy making his mark and a rising star in the ranks—rumors started and pictures that seemed to back them up began. The tabloids followed him and his brothers everywhere now that they were billionaires, gorgeous, and single. The Tanner brothers were news, and Bret, with his NFR dreams within his grasp, was prime target number one.

Her mouth was dirt-dry as she spotted him in the back of the building. She wished for a glass of water with lemon because her voice was going to crack when she tried to speak to him for that first time. When stressed, she was prone to losing her voice. And today she was highly stressed.

She sometimes broke out in hives and she prayed today was not the day for that. As an entertainment reporter, she often had to speak to high-profile individuals. But none of them filled her with anxiety like approaching Bret Tanner did. Too much history. Too many heartaches stretched between them now.

Appear calm, cool, and collected. Right—she needed to put on the show of her life. Bret Tanner did not need to know that he had broken her heart all those years ago or that she had never recovered from seeing him on the cover of all those tabloids with different women while she'd been here in their hometown waiting on him. Oh, he'd denied the photos were true, but she'd grown tired of the constant heartache.

All she needed from him today was an interview. An interview that her job depended on. Readership was down, and her boss had found out she knew the billionaire, two-time NFR champion and six-time finalist. She had to act as if their past was in the past and he hadn't hurt her. When in truth she had never recovered from loving him, despite all the women he'd had in his life. This was make it or break it. No pressure.

None at all.

Taking a deep breath, she walked forward.

* * *

Bret Tanner sat at the back table in the shadows of Manny's Bar and Grill, waiting on his brother Jake to join him. Jake had walked in the door a few minutes earlier and had stopped across the room to talk to someone he knew. Bret sat in the dimmest corner in the joint, hoping to have a quiet dinner with his brother.

He was in town for a big event to raise money for a new children's wing of the hospital in San Antonio. He liked to use his notoriety to benefit causes he cared about in any way he could, especially when it involved something to help children. For this, he would gladly put on his Stetson and be the pro bull rider persona to raise money. And because of the amount of money his family had made a few years back when one of the largest oil strikes in Texas history blasted them into billionaire status, they also had the means to help in their chosen avenues of causes they believed in. There were a lot of weird drawbacks to that money coming into their lives, but there were also too many benefits to ignore now that he'd matured and wasn't resentful of the way the media had hounded him and his brothers over the years.

They'd all started focusing on the good they could do with the money and not the negative ways it had taken their quiet cowboy, ranching way of life and transformed it into a circus at times. So this was an idea that Tulip and Cole had come up with and were hosting the event at the Tanner main ranch, where they lived. They were showcasing the beautiful gardens that their mother had started and that Tulip had taken to the next level when she'd come to the ranch. They had pulled him into the event easily because he loved helping kids. It should be a successful fundraiser; there would be a lot of wealthy people at the event who were willing and wanting to help raise money to help the children's hospital wing.

It was also going to be an event that would enable

certain types of businesses in the area to showcase their goods. Rita, Levi's wife, was a photographer who had recently opened a photography/wedding planning venue in Fredericksburg. A True Love florist would also be donating her time, creating photo-worthy backdrops for the guests to have their photos taken, while also giving both women a chance to showcase their small businesses.

He was glad it had worked out and he didn't have a rodeo for seven days. He had just flown into town two days earlier. He still had five days before he hit the road again, and the charity was in three. He wasn't a huge fan of dressing in fancy clothes, but he did it for good causes. He'd dressed up recently for his brother Cole's wedding and again for Levi's wedding—both good causes—and he was glad for them. Afterward, they'd both asked him what his plan was. When was he going to get married? Not anytime soon. Love hadn't worked out for him. And he hadn't been in any hurry for a repeat of that disaster.

Nope, he had his heart broken once and hadn't opened his heart again since. Only to family and rodeo and helping kids…but a woman? Not a chance.

Rodeo gave him purpose. He watched the condensation on his glass of iced water—his drink of choice. Unlike many of his competitors, Bret took extreme care of what he put into his body in order to keep it at maximum performance. Rodeo was hard enough without adding to the problem. He ran a finger along the dampness and glanced toward Jake, who was still talking. Bret let his gaze wander the room as his thoughts churned, now having snagged on his love of rodeo and the ever-present realization that his love affair with rodeo, specifically bull riding, couldn't last forever, no matter how close he watched his diet or kept in shape. Bull riding was hard on the body, and there was no getting around that fact. The reality was he would have to give it up at some point. Living on the road was hard, and as much as he hated the idea of giving up competing, he was growing weary of being on the road. Living on the blacktop, as some would say. But could he be satisfied without the adrenaline rush and competition he loved? When he gave it up, then what?

He tried not to let his mood slide downward and pushed the thoughts away, but they kept coming back, stronger and stronger. No amount of denial was going to stop the facts from playing out. His career was riding high right now, despite multiple injuries plaguing him, and he'd worked hard to hold onto his position in this year's standings. But for how long?

His body hurt right now from a particularly rough ride. He boarded the charter plane after the rodeo and taken three over-the-counter painkillers—stopping just short of pulling out the prescription pain meds he carried in his bag for when the ride was too rough to handle. Lately, he'd been taking the prescription meds more than he cared to, a testament to the fact that his body was not handling his beloved profession as well as it once had.

He'd fallen into bed at Jake's place and been dead to the world until a rooster started crowing a few hours later. His pain meds had worn off by then, so he'd rolled out of bed and found Jake in the kitchen, making coffee. He'd gratefully accepted the freshly brewed mug of coffee, grabbed an icepack from the freezer and began icing down his shoulder while he drank his coffee. He'd been icing down his shoulder all day and hoped tomorrow would be better. But it was just one more sign that the inevitable was coming and he was going to have to stop avoiding the reality.

His gaze roamed around the dining room when, on the far side of the room, the front door of Manny's opened, and a slender woman was silhouetted in the light. She wore a white blouse and a black skirt, a tight-fitting skirt that wasn't too short or too long, hitting just above her knees. Looked like a skirt to a business suit. She walked into the room and he watched her say something to the hostess, then move toward the back of the room where he and many others were sitting.

The light was too dim and he was too far away to see her features, but something about the way she moved was familiar. She stopped and scanned the room, seeming familiar with her surroundings as she pushed a strand of shoulder-length black hair behind her ear and then stepped into the light.

He inhaled sharply. *Ellie.*

It had been a long time and the odds were always against him when he came home to True Love; it was a small place. But they hadn't run into each other in nearly six years. He picked up his water and took a drink, his mouth suddenly dry. His stomach burned, and he kept his gaze on her as she continued to come his way. He knew that she could not see him, the lights were too dim, and his hat was pulled too low over his eyes anyway. Yet, she approached as though she knew exactly where she was going.

Memories shot through him at that moment of another time when the two of them sat in a booth at the back, his arm around her as he'd steal a kiss. *He'd loved kissing her.*

He shut that thought down as his stomach knotted and dread rose with each step she took.

She filled that prim business attire out very nicely, although he preferred her in jeans and the frilly tops she'd loved when they were younger. And why was he thinking about Ellie Seton and the way they'd been? It was not a good thing to travel down that long-ago road to heartache.

This woman was sleek, not the sweet cowgirl he'd once thought hung the moon. His heart raged as her gaze locked onto his.

Those beautiful lavender eyes still haunted his days and nights when his guard was down. Not soft and lovely and inviting, they now looked harsh. *What was up with that?* He sat up straighter and then he told himself to relax; if she was coming his way, he didn't need to act as if he cared. He slouched a little bit, picked up his water, and took a sip as she walked right up to his table. His heart began beating with the horsepower of a NASCAR stock car.

"Hello, Bret," she said in that soft, husky voice of hers that used to push all his buttons.

He didn't move his gaze away from her. "Ellie. What brings you to town?" He sounded harsh, bitter, and he didn't like it. He wanted to be over her. Wanted her to believe he was, no matter whether he was or wasn't.

"Actually, I came to see you," she said hesitantly.

Her words rammed into him as if somebody had just hit him with a sledgehammer, or he had gotten kicked by a bunch of stampeding stallions.

"Me? Why are you here to see me? We finished our business a long time ago."

She shifted from one red high heel to the other and pushed her hair behind her ear again.

He wished the flickering light on his table was a little brighter so he could see what those eyes of hers were saying, but he couldn't.

"I need to talk to you. Do you have a minute?"

"I'm here with Jake and after that, we're supposed to meet up with Levi and Cole soon."

She looked disappointed as she remained ramrod straight. "I see. Could we meet tomorrow then? I'm going to help Mom some with the flowers for the benefit that Cole and your family is hosting at the main ranch. I can work around any time you have available. I might even be out at the ranch at some point to look at where the arrangements will be."

Dread filled him. *She was helping her mom with the flowers.* "I heard your mom was doing the flowers. I didn't know you were helping her, though." He sounded less than enthusiastic but he didn't care. He was not planning to spend time around her. And why was she wanting to meet with him, anyway?

"I wasn't supposed to, but I was here, so I've offered to help, and she accepted my help. She was a bit overwhelmed, I think, by the amount of arrangements. It's going to be gorgeous."

"That's what Mom and Dad said. Levi's new wife, Rita, is really going all out on the decorations, and that makes more flowers to do for your mom."

"Yes, but she's all in. She's planning to expand her business if there is a good reaction. Which is what Rita, with her wedding photography and wedding planning business, is anticipating."

"That's what I've been told."

"So, can we meet tomorrow?"

What was the deal? "I'm going to be real busy helping set up. Why do you need to talk to me?"

She took a deep breath, and he could tell she was not liking this any more than he was. *So what was up?*

"I'd rather talk to you about it in private not just blurt it out right here. But it's important and I'd appreciate it very much."

"Okay, I'll meet you. Where?"

"How about the river?"

"The river. Okay." Why had he agreed to the river, of all places? There were a lot of long, curvy rivers in the Hill Country that wove all through the countryside, and yet he knew exactly where she meant for him to meet her.

They'd met many times at the spot they'd once called "their" spot before everything changed.

"Great. Ten?"

"I'll see you there." He just wanted her to leave now. He spotted Jake and others watching them.

"Then I guess I'll be going." She spun away and walked back the way she'd come in, not nearly as slowly as she'd approached him. She was trying to get out as fast as she could.

And, to his horror, it took everything in him not to run after her.

Thankfully, Jake finally came over and took a seat across from him. His little brother was grinning like an opossum as he watched the door close behind the love of Bret's life.

"What was that all about?" Jake asked as the waitress came to get their order.

Bret no longer had an appetite. *What did she want after all this time?* The blast from the past had set him on edge. When asked, he gave his order to the waitress, who took his order and then blushed as she took Jake's order. His brother proceeded to spend a moment flirting with her, and the interaction gave Bret a moment to adjust his attitude. His family didn't know how hard he'd taken the breakup with Ellie. He didn't want them or anyone knowing that he still hadn't gotten over what Ellie had done to him all those years ago.

It was pathetic that he couldn't move on completely. There were times he thought he'd managed it, then he would see an article she'd written, or he would glimpse her somewhere in town on the few times they were both home during a holiday. It was always from a distance, because he was always on the lookout for her and tried to avoid her at all costs. Even going as far as the first few years of just not coming home when he knew she was likely to be in town.

But nobody needed to know it. He was the brother who had it all—had his dream come true. He was riding high in the NFR; he had only won it those first two years, but he was always in the top six. And this year, he was the one to beat. He just had to get there in December and make it happen. He was the brother with the boyish looks who seemed to never be disturbed by anything. He had a very good poker face. And that's the way he wanted to keep it.

After the waitress walked away with their orders, Jake settled back in his chair. "Was that a fan you were talking to? It looked interesting." He grinned.

"Just somebody wanting to talk to me."

"For an interview, an autograph, or a date?"

"I don't know." His head was so screwed up right now, and he knew it was futile to not say it was Ellie. It wasn't going to take Jake long to figure it out, anyway. "It wasn't important."

Jake's gaze dug into him and Bret tried his hardest to keep his poker face in place.

"You know I can tell you're lying, right?"

"I'm not lying." Frustration riffled through him and settled in his gut. He slapped his elbows onto the plank tabletop and cupped his hands together. Leaning forward, he frowned. "Okay, if you must know, it was Ellie Seton."

Jake's expression went from shock to a grin. "Ellie. Wow. I don't think you've seen her in a long time, have you?"

"Nope. I haven't. And I hadn't expected to see her tonight. It was a shock when she came over to my table."

"I know you two broke up on bad terms and I know you avoid talking about it at all cost, but it seems like y'all should be over it. You don't seem over it."

"I'm over it. I just don't like thinking about her."

"You don't look over it. You were in love with her. We all thought you two were going to get married."

"You thought wrong."

Jake's gaze narrowed. "I hear she's doing great."

"Maybe. I don't know. I don't keep up with her. But yeah, I cared for her a long time ago and she broke it off."

"Maybe she's ready to give it another go."

"I'm not. That ship sailed a long time ago."

"You sure are touchy."

"Can we drop this? I'm not interested. Burn me once—not going to get a chance to burn me twice."

"Totally agree with you on that. So, why was she here?"

He shot his brother a scowl. "I don't know. I'm going to meet her tomorrow and find out, okay? Is that fine with you?"

Jake held his hands up. "Hey, I'm just asking. Relax. You're wound up like a ball of barbed wire. I think she got to you more than you're admitting."

"I wasn't expecting her to walk in. I hadn't seen or heard from her since she called me right before my first National Finals ride and broke up with me, so let's just say I'm not thrilled to see her."

"I'm on your side. I can get why you're upset. But if something like this has got you so twisted up inside like you are right now, maybe it's time to figure out why." Jake was right.

Their food was delivered, and he stared at it, not hungry at all. Despite his reluctance about the meeting tomorrow, they did need to talk.

CHAPTER TWO

Ellie's hands shook as she twisted the key and the car engine purred to life. "Why did I agree to do this?" she muttered as she glanced in the rearview and then backed out of the parking space. Breathing hard and fighting back the emotions trying to overtake her, she rammed the gearshift into drive and pressed the pedal. The sooner she was away from here, the better.

Moments later, as she drove down the dark country road toward her parents' home, she had forced herself to calm down. She was not an over-the-top, emotional mess normally, and she had no plans to become one now. Especially not because of Bret.

Yes, age had been good to him. His dark good looks were still there, and those bright eyes that had always been so expressive and enticing were just as expressive and enticing as ever. But there was an edge to them now. Maybe it was simply that she'd startled him when she'd walked straight up to him with no warning. Maybe that closed-up shadow of caution and wariness was only for her. Maybe, even after all these years, he still believed she'd been the bad guy, breaking up with him after promising to wait.

She drove into the driveway of her parents' home. Her mother's home now that her dad had died, something she still couldn't get used to. She'd expected to hear him greet her earlier today when she'd walked into the house and called out hello. When her smiling mother had rounded the corner alone and grabbed her up in a bear hug, she'd been so happy to see her but at the same time felt the loss of her dad deeply.

Maybe one day she'd get used to it, but she couldn't imagine that day ever coming.

"Honey," her mom called the minute she walked in the garage door. "Wash up. I've got dinner on the table."

She closed her eyes and paused in the hall. She had no appetite but couldn't disappoint her mom. "I'll be right there. It smells delicious." And it did. Definitely something with Italian seasoning, and considering this was her first evening back, it had to be her favorite: homemade beef ravioli smothered in Italian marinara sauce. She would have to eat something, or her mom would know something was bothering her. She'd never been able to say no to ravioli.

She washed her hands and dried them as she stared at herself in the mirror. She pinched her cheeks, trying to get some color into them, and then headed down the hall to the kitchen.

"Have a seat at the bar. I already set the plates out. It's so nice to have someone to eat with while you're home. You know your dad always wanted to sit down together."

She sank onto the cushioned barstool. "I miss him."

"I do too. He'd be happy right now that you are here. Just like I am. I made your favorite."

She smiled, feeling better just by being here. "I hoped that was what I smelled. I can't wait."

"Then after I say the blessing you can dig in."

Her mother took a seat beside her. They automatically clasped hands and bowed their heads as her mom said a prayer of thanksgiving for the food and for Ellie being there with her and spending some time at home.

Ellie let the peace of that moment sink in and wrap itself around her. She was home, and her mother's presence steadied her, and the prayer reminded her that no matter what might happen, she could make it through. Even the meeting tomorrow with Bret.

Tonight was about her mom and this welcome home meal made especially for her.

"Now, is everything all right? Linda Dingle called and said she saw you and Bret talking at Manny's. That must have been a shock but I'm glad you saw each other before the benefit. Maybe things won't be so awkward. How did you know he was there?"

"It was awkward but I need to get an interview with him while I'm home. I just happened to see him drive through town as I was leaving the gas station. I decided to follow him and old habits don't die. He always did love to eat at Manny's."

"You did, too."

"Yes, but it's been a very long time since I set foot in there."

"Did you set up a meeting with him?"

"I did. He was reluctant but agreed. I'm meeting with him before I come to the flower shop in the morning."

Her mother's eyes lit up. "Great. Take all the time you need."

She didn't have the heart to tell her mother that she fully expected Bret to turn her down flat once he knew what she needed from him.

* * *

The next morning, Bret parked his truck beside the red rental and stared at the path through the trees. He took a deep breath, hung his head, and told himself to get hold of himself. Seeing her the night before had turned every moment since into turmoil.

He stepped out onto the dirt, closed the truck's door and then paused, staring at the opening in the trees and the path to the river. How many times had he walked down that path to meet Ellie when they were younger? Too many to count. It had been their special place.

Get on with it.

"Yeah, let it go," he growled under his breath, then strode toward the path. Heart pounding, he wound through the trees down to the river. Obviously, others still used this path as it was still visible, with only some groundcover in patches. He saw her sitting on the big rock that protruded over the water. His mouth went dry and his gut ached as if he had eaten bad eggs. He stuffed a hand in his pocket and then walked forward.

She heard him, somehow, even over the soft sound of the river. This area of the river was just so peaceful. The trees probably rose up twenty-five feet or so from the ridge, towering above the lower embankment that he walked toward. It was a very shaded area, remote and beautiful. The river widened here, creating an area to swim in. There used to be a rope swing that hung from one of the trees. They'd loved to swing from a rock and drop into the cool water. It had been fun, and part of many good memories here. Why had she chosen this spot for their meeting? The swing was long gone, as well as the good memories they'd shared here.

Why hadn't she chosen a neutral place? When they were here, they had often been in each other's arms. They'd spent many hours talking about their future…their plan for him to be a rodeo champion and her to be a stay-at-home mom so she could travel with him as much as possible. That had been her dream. She'd just wanted to be his wife and mother of his children. She'd wanted to love him and make a home for them.

And then she'd walked away and chosen a career in journalism.

Bitterness hardened his heart as that night slammed into him. The night she'd called him and tossed their dreams aside.

Too much time had passed; this was not a path he needed to stroll down again.

"Hey." Her voice sounded a little bit breathless,

like she was nervous too. She stood beside the river and shifted from one foot to the other. She wore black leggings, pink jogging shoes, and a silky white blouse that hung mid-thigh.

"Hey," he grunted. He chose to remain standing at the path's edge. He crossed his arms and waited.

She swallowed and moistened her lips.

His gaze followed the movement, then shot back to her eyes. He focused on her eyes, holding his gaze steady. But even that was hard. Her lavender eyes were big and full of some kind of emotion that he did not want to think about—because it looked as if she were thinking about how it used to be when they came here.

"I don't have all day. I have to get back and help decorate for the benefit." He knew he was being gruff, but he couldn't take this.

"Right. I'm here because I've been assigned to interview you. I know that's probably the last thing you thought I'd say, but my boss found out that I knew you and gave me the assignment. He thought a personalized interview from one of the top-ranking rodeo champions would be a good fit for the series on athletes from all the different sports."

He stared at her, not believing his ears. "I'm home for this cancer benefit. I'm not here to give interviews." And not to her, anyway. He had no plans to sit down and give a personalized interview with the woman who had stomped on his heart and walked away.

"That's what I thought you would say." She looked away from him and stared at the river. For a moment, she looked lost.

He did not need to be thinking about her being lost or vulnerable. He would not fall for that. He just stood there, wanting to turn away and jog back up the hill, get in his truck and drive away.

She nodded toward the water. "Water's still pretty as always. We had some good times here, didn't we?"

Now she was going to use their history against him. Anger boiled up inside him. "Yeah, we did. A long time ago. Why in the world did you pick this place to have a meeting?"

"I don't know. When you asked me where we wanted to meet, it was the first thing that popped into my head. I guess because this is where we always came. It was a reaction. Now I see it wasn't a good choice."

"Nope." He wrapped a hand around the back of his neck and rubbed the tension building there. "Well, I've got work to do." He turned and started back up the trail.

"Bret!"

He stopped, hung his head, and told himself to just keep walking. He didn't owe her anything. But he had never been a jerk and he'd been feeling like one from the moment she'd walked up to his table last night. He turned slowly, hating himself as he fought the feelings threatening to break down the barriers he'd built around his heart. He would not, could not give in to the longing to take her into his arms and kiss her. He'd thought about that all night long.

He'd had plans for a future with Ellie, and she'd tossed him away. He'd still loved her when she'd called him that night. And he feared he still did.

Taking her in as he turned back to face her, he knew he still had a weakness for her. Knew that, after all these years, it was still there.

He swallowed hard. His mouth was as dry as a desert storm. "What?"

"I know we didn't end well. But I'm sure your mother would say we need to move past that, just as my mother has said to me. Since they are such good friends, they do discuss our past. Maybe we do need to get this out in the open. Maybe me interviewing you could help us figure out a way to do that. At least be able to get to a point where we don't avoid each other when we come back to town. Because we both know we do that. I know I hurt you, and surely you know you hurt me. But it was a long time ago. We need to let it go."

He stared at her. He couldn't move. *She thought they could do an interview, and everything would be hunky-dory, okay, back to normal?*

"I don't exactly know what you're talking about," he hedged, or just flat out lied—because he knew exactly what she was talking about. But if he acknowledged that, he would be showing her how much she'd hurt him. And he didn't want anyone, especially her, knowing she'd ripped his heart out.

She sighed. "Fine. So you want to play that game. Look, I hate admitting this, but if I don't get this interview, I'm going to lose my job."

He clinched his jaw at the disclosure, that she would seek him out and use that to get at him. "I'm not sure how your job came to hang on the balance of an interview with me, but that's too bad because I'm not doing an interview with you. You'll find another job, I'm sure." Turning away, he shut down any guilt tugging at him. He owed her nothing. Not one blasted thing.

He started back up that hill and this time he ignored her when she called out for him to wait. His hands shook when he slid behind the wheel of his truck and twisted the key. He was headed back toward town within seconds, his mind reeling from the meeting with Ellie. Agreeing to the meeting ranked up there as one of the worst decisions he had ever made.

He should have said no way right from the start.

* * *

Ellie couldn't move. She stared at the spot in the trees

where Bret had been standing before he'd walked away so coldly. He had turned into a hard man.

He had acted so cold last night, and this had not helped the situation. She'd known deep down this would be the outcome.

She raked a hand through her black hair as she turned to stare at the flowing river. Her knees wobbled and she sank down onto a rock. Drawing her knees up, she wrapped her arms around them and rocked gently back and forth. *She was going to lose her job.*

She should have accepted the fact and never even approached Bret.

The sooner she came to grips with that, the better. She should have just admitted that before she'd come here. Why had she even thought that he would care? Why had she even thought that they could overcome their past? It had been too hard seeing him, anyway. He looked so good to her and, despite the years that had passed, it hurt to look at him. It hurt, thinking about what they could have had.

They could have already started a family. She had dreamed of having a family with Bret. She had even named their children. Three of them, three adorable little cherub-faced children that she'd given both a boy name and a girl name as she had no preference on gender. She just wanted to be a mother to Bret's babies.

Instead of a marriage or a family, she'd had a career.

And she'd done really well with it. And now she was about to lose that. Life was not turning out how she thought it would. And just like the fast-moving water of the river, her life was swiftly moving on. As she stared at the water, a huge buck with a giant rack of horns strode majestically down the ravine on the other side of the river from where she sat. Stunned, Ellie froze. He was beautiful and, even more to her surprise, he paused at the water's edge and stared at her.

She barely inhaled, so afraid she would scare him, and he would bolt away. Her heart hammered. She wanted a photo so badly but knew he would run back into the woods, so she just sat there. The sound of the water rushing along between them and the occasional call of a bird were the only sounds as they held each other's stare. Tears welled in her eyes, realizing just how precious a moment this was. And then, he lifted his chin, spun, and in powerful, graceful strides, he bolted up the embankment and disappeared over the ridge.

She exhaled slowly, her breath trembling. She blinked away the tears, knowing this was a moment she would never forget. And a sad reminder to her that God gave precious moments in life and none of them were to be taken for granted.

All those years ago, had she given up on her and Bret too soon? Had she destroyed what they'd had because she'd been impatient? Or jealous? Or just plain too young to know how to fight for what she'd wanted?

If she had harbored any small subconscious hope of reconciling with Bret, that was gone, and she knew it. Nothing of the sort would ever come to fruition. She blinked hard against a sudden urge to cry. She might as well pack her bags and head out today.

But where would she go?

Back to Houston to start looking for another job? She could do that here.

At least the longer she stayed here, the longer her job held out. The longer she had to figure out a way to salvage the situation. She needed her boss to think she was at least making progress. And who knew? A miracle could happen over the weekend with the benefit. Her mother needed her to help with the flowers she'd be doing, and had asked her to chip in and help.

It felt devious and yet she could give it a few more days.

CHAPTER THREE

By the time Ellie drove back into town, she was calmer. She'd gotten her thoughts together. She would remain here for the week and help her mom with the flowers, and she might run into Bret a few times. When the time presented itself, she would ask him again for an interview. She hadn't gotten to where she was today in her career without being tenacious, and that meant that as much as she hated asking him again, she would.

She parked in front of her mother's small florist, Seton Designs. She had opened this florist when Ellie had been in junior high school, and Ellie had grown up amid beautiful flowers and floral arrangements. Ellie had worked for her mom through high school, and she'd turned out to be a natural at creating floral arrangements.

After Bret had broken her heart, she'd needed to get away from True Love. Before she'd fallen for him, she'd wanted to be a writer and have a career in journalism but had gone to work for her mom instead, putting off college. So, with a heavy heart, she'd gone after that old dream.

Her mother had carried on without her, building her shop's reputation up and staying busy with the floral needs of the area.

When Levi Tanner's new bride, Rita, opened a photography/wedding business in Fredericksburg, she saw some of Betty's creations and loved her arrangements and invited her to do the benefit with her. They were going to be Western dried flower and fresh flowering Texas wildflower combinations, something that happened to be her mother's specialty. Ellie had become quite proficient herself at arranging all manner of flowers around Texas symbols: boots, cattle horns, lassoes, and spurs—all kinds of things that said authentic Texas with a Western flair. In this part of the country, it was a theme that never grew old but could always have a twist of creativity that made it new and fresh. Her mother had that knack.

Ellie climbed out of her car and stepped onto the sidewalk. Through the glass, she spotted her mom standing mid-way up on the ladder that slid along a rail, giving her access to the high shelves where she stored some of her vases and baskets. Ellie always worried about her mother climbing on that ladder. The doorbell chimed as she walked inside.

"Oh, good, Ellie. You're just in time." Holding a huge wicker basket in her arms, her mother smiled down at her. "I'm about to make an arrangement in this basket. Can you get this for me?" She leaned down and lowered the basket.

Ellie hurried forward. "Mom, I think you need to move all that stuff down a little bit. I'm so worried you're going to fall off that thing. I've always been worried about it."

Betty laughed. "I've only fallen once. And I was not hurt." As if fate was laughing at them, her mother's foot slipped on the third rung as she stepped down on it. One moment, she was handing Ellie the basket; the next, she fell backward.

Ellie let the basket fall and reached for her mother, grabbing her shoulder just before her mother landed on the ground. It didn't do much good but it kept her mother's head from slamming on the floor.

She cried out in pain when she landed.

Ellie dropped to the floor beside her. "Mom, lay still. Don't move. I've got to call someone."

Her mom stared at her, pain on her face. "Thank you for grabbing my shoulder. I didn't hit my head, thank goodness. I guess I shouldn't have said anything about not falling off the ladder before. Goes to show me." She grunted the words out as her face hitched into a grimace.

"Where do you hurt?"

"Oh, my hip and my ankle."

Ellie looked behind her and realized her mom's foot was still caught in the first rung, somehow having slipped through it as she fell. "Don't move. Your ankle may be sprained or could be that it's broken. Let me get help. Just don't move. Lay back—lay your head down. It will be okay. Your hip's worrying me, too."

Jumping up, she yanked her phone from her purse and dialed…who did she need to call? Her brain swirled. Without hesitation, after her brain hit on Bret, she dialed the number.

Bret answered, "Hello, Ellie? Did you forget to tell me something?" His voice was not eager to hear from her but at this moment she didn't care.

"Bret, is Austin around? Is he off today? Or is he working?"

"He took a few days off to help with the benefit."

"My mom has fallen at the florist. I didn't know whether to call 911, or I thought if he was at the ranch, he could get here quicker."

"Is she talking?"

"Yes, but she hit the ground hard, and her hip and ankle are hurt. I was able to grab her shoulder and keep her head from hitting the ground but she's hurting. I don't know… I wasn't sure—"

"We're on our way. I'll call you back as soon as we're rolling your way. He'll tell you whether to call 911 or not."

"Thank you." She hung up. Her heart pounded, feeling more unsteady than she had felt in a very long time. It hit her that she hadn't really ever dealt with an emergency like this. Her heart was palpitating like crazy and she felt weak. Her head spun a little bit and she could hyperventilate if she couldn't get a hold of herself. This was her mom. Her mom was hurting. And it could have been worse. She hurried to the seating area to the side and grabbed a pillow from one of the seats.

"I'm going to slip this under your head." She gently slipped the pillow under her head. "Relax and try not to move. Austin is on his way, and he'll know how to fix you up. I thought he could get here faster than an ambulance."

"You did right. I don't think we need an ambulance. Austin'll know what to do. He's a wonderful doctor. I've heard that he is great in an emergency. I think that's what he loves to do, mostly…work the emergency room." She shifted and gasped.

"Take it easy." Ellie patted her mom's arm and

prayed Bret and Austin would get there soon. She was trying not to panic but this was her mother, and Ellie hated to see the brave face she was putting on when Ellie could see the pain in her eyes.

* * *

"I didn't even know Ellie was in town," Austin said after Bret had grabbed him from where he was helping set poles for the awning Rita had asked to be built as a backdrop of photos for the guests at the event.

"I just found out last night. She came into Manny's. First time I've talked to her in years. I hope Betty is okay."

"I do too, so get me there. I hate the idea of her mom lying on the floor, hurting. I'll call her while you're driving and get a handle on the situation."

Bret gunned the engine of his truck as he turned off the ranch's driveway onto the blacktop road and headed toward town. Hill Country wasn't the best place to get somewhere fast but he had grown up on these roads; he knew where every curve was. He knew where to slow down and speed up, and he concentrated on that while Austin used his phone to call Ellie back and ask questions about her mom. He felt bad for Betty, Ellie's mom. He prayed she wasn't hurt too bad. Ellie had sounded upset, but at least it was her hip or ankle and not her head. Thankfully she had been there to help break her mother's fall.

There was a part of him that wanted to get there to see whether he could comfort her in some way. He called himself all kinds of a fool because of those feelings. Their history was so mixed up, complicated, and so convoluted. His heart was tangled like a cow stuck in a barbed-wire fence after having been through so many different emotions where Ellie was concerned. And yet he had the gas pedal to the floor of the truck as they hit the straightaway into town and the urgency to get to her, to help her mother, could not be denied.

They were close to town when Austin ended his call with Ellie. "We're dealing with a hip and ankle injury. Let's pray it's a bruised hip and not a break. The ankle, I believe, could be a bad sprain. I'm putting a call in for an ambulance."

Bret prayed for the bruised hip scenario rather than a break as he listened to Austin calling for the ambulance. They reached True Love, and Bret pulled to a halt in front of the florist shop, parking beside the Ellie's car. Both of them barreled out of the truck and into the shop at a run.

Ellie sat on the floor beside Betty, holding her hand, looking pale and distressed. Her mother clearly was in pain but gave them a goodhearted smile as they crouched down beside them.

"Hey, boys. Thanks for coming. I was clumsy and have my girl here scared to death."

Austin placed a hand of comfort on Ellie's shoulder. "You two have been through it. Hang in there a little longer. Ambulance is on the way but, in the meantime, let's have a look."

Bret knelt on the other side of Betty and felt out of place. "You're going to be all right, Ms. Seton. You're a tough lady." Bret gave her a smile of encouragement and then met Ellie's gaze. Guilt twisted in his gut at their morning meeting just an hour ago. It seemed almost a lifetime ago suddenly.

Austin began doing an assessment, moving his hands along her hip and ankle. He touched her hip, leg, and ankle, asking questions and seeing what they were dealing with.

Bret could see Ellie was really worried and when Austin touched her mother's hip and she flinched hard and groaned, Ellie flinched too. He felt for both of them.

"She wasn't hurting quite that bad at first, but it seems like it's getting worse," Ellie told Austin.

"We'll take her in for some X-rays. It could be a major contusion and not a break, but we still need to check it out. As for your ankle, I'm pretty sure it's a sprain. The ambulance should be here any minute. I know you're in pain but once they get here, we'll get that taken care of. You're a good trooper. Were you reaching for those baskets and those vases up there?"

"I've done it for years." Betty sighed.

"And I've worried about it for years," Ellie added.

"I'd say you've been lucky for years. Maybe Ellie can rearrange things so you don't need those shelves."

"I can help," Bret offered without hesitation, grasping at the opportunity to help this lady who was one of his mother's best friends and who had always been nice to him. And to make an effort to make up for being so rude earlier to Ellie.

"I can do it," Ellie said, not looking at him.

Betty grunted in pain, closed her eyes, and nodded. It was easy for them all to see she was fighting the pain.

Ellie patted her hand, and he wanted to put his hand on her shoulder and give support, but he didn't.

The ambulance could be heard; sirens blasted as it turned the corner and drew closer and closer, flying down the main street of True Love. Two seconds later, it was parked outside, lights still flashing but the siren off. The EMTs jumped out, came in, and took over. They moved out of the way, standing to the side as the medical team worked on her.

He crossed his arms, and Ellie wrapped her arms around herself as she watched.

"She's going to be okay. You know they're going to take good care of your mom."

"Thanks for coming. I didn't know what else to do. I couldn't decide whether to call 911 and then I realized that Austin might be there, so I called you."

"Working the shifts he works, he has weird hours, being on call at the emergency room and then working it so much. You made a good call."

She looked at him, their eyes holding. She nodded and her gaze darted back to her mom as they lifted her onto the gurney.

He could tell she wanted to move back over there but knew she would just be in the way so, against everything in him, he placed his hand on her shoulder that was closest to him. He didn't wrap his arm around her; he patted the shoulder next to him. It was kind of awkward. "It will be okay."

She looked at him. "Thanks. Thanks for coming."

They wheeled her mom past them, out on to the sidewalk and then the pavement, then lifted the gurney into the back of the ambulance.

"Are you riding with her?" an EMT asked.

She looked at Austin and then back at them. "Can Austin ride?"

Austin rubbed her arm. "Why don't you ride with her, and I'll have Bret follow you. We'll be right behind y'all."

"Okay. As long as you think she's out of danger."

"I think she's out of danger as far as an emergency happening."

She nodded, put the closed sign up, and locked up the shop, then climbed inside with her mom. She took her hand as they closed the door of the ambulance.

Austin looked at Bret. "You ready to drive me? You look pretty stunned and upset yourself."

"Let's go. It's just, you know, our history. We've been estranged for years, so it makes this real confusing now."

Austin clapped him on the back. "Yeah, I can see that. I've let you deal privately with the breakup like you seemed to want, but I was surprised that you two didn't end up together. Maybe this is a second chance to give y'all an opportunity to connect and move forward. At least to get more comfortable around each other."

Bret pressed the gas and caught up with the

ambulance. "As far as I'm concerned, there's no need for a second chance. I ride bulls for a living—I know what getting your heart and your body stomped on feels like. And the hit to the heart when she broke up with me was worse than any beating by a bull I've ever had. That's not going to happen again."

CHAPTER FOUR

They were in the emergency room waiting area, and Ellie was very thankful that Austin had come to her mom's rescue along with the ambulance. And Bret, too. Standing by the window, her arms wrapped tightly together, she waited for him to come back from getting them both a cup of coffee. He had been very kind since they had arrived and were now waiting on Austin to come back and let them know what the verdict was about her mother. She had to admit it was nice not to be waiting alone. But it was very awkward.

"Here you go. Two creams and one sugar, just like you like."

She turned at his voice and accepted the Styrofoam cup of coffee he extended to her. She noticed he was careful to stay almost at arm's length away from her. She accepted the coffee, trying to ignore the stirring inside her chest when their fingers brushed. There would be none of that. And why was she feeling anything, anyway? She was worried about her mother. *Fickle insides.*

"Thank you. I don't know what I need more—the caffeine from the coffee or the punch the sugar will give me. But the combination's perfect." She took the coffee then let the steam and the scent rise up; she breathed it in before testing it with a small sip. Thankfully, it was hot and sweet. She welcomed the adrenaline shot it gave her. She had been feeling very unsteady, as if maybe she were having a low blood sugar thing or something. She'd lost her dad two years earlier when he'd been hit by a falling limb while cutting down a tree, and now her mother's accident had hit her hard.

"You're welcome. You look pretty pale—maybe that will give you a jolt. I can go get you something to eat." He looked worried about her. "I got you this just in case you wouldn't let me." He pulled a package of

Hostess white powdered donuts from his shirt pocket. "I know how you used to love these things. It will give you a little energy."

The fact that he remembered how much she loved the sugary donuts made her smile. She took the package from him and sat down in the chair behind her.

He remained standing.

She looked up at him. "I'll share." She set her coffee down in the cup holder on the chair's arm and then fumbled with the package. It wouldn't open.

He sat down beside her and then gently took the package from her. "Let me."

She tried to ignore how the brush of his fingers against hers made her feel. "Thank you."

He smiled and tugged the package open, then gave it back to her.

She picked one out and then offered the opened bag to him.

"Thanks." He took one, popped the entire donut into his mouth, and grinned.

She took a bite and let the sweetness soak through

her, giving her some bit of comfort. Then she sobered. "Bret, you should have seen her fall. Her head would have hit that hard floor and who knows how bad that could have been. I just had time to reach out and grab her shoulder and hold on tight to her shirt. That was the only thing that saved her from slamming her shoulder and head against that floor. She fell so hard that it yanked me forward and I just held on so tight." She blinked back tears as the emotions that had eluded her while trying to be strong, waiting for them to get there and take care of her mom, started to take hold.

"Understandable. But you were there for her, so I'd say the Lord was looking out for your mom today. You being home, and her not falling from as high as she could have fallen—that right there is amazing in itself."

She took a breath and nodded. She needed something to keep the tears at bay, so she picked her hot cup of coffee up and took a sip, letting the heat burn through her, giving her a little more stability on her emotions. "I haven't been home in a while, and I'm glad I was here too." She took another bite, not really knowing what to say to him now that they'd gotten all the easy, obvious things out there. With all her fear and her worry, she was grateful to have somebody to share it with, but Bret of all people was the hardest one to share it with. To let him see all the emotion and the fear that had gripped her. Now, if she wasn't talking about the fear, what else could she talk to him about? How much she really needed his interview—an interview that, at the moment, she couldn't care less about because she was so worried about her mom.

"Will your mom be able to make it if her injury stops her from working?"

Ellie dropped her head back and closed her eyes as the power of his words sank over her and curdled in her stomach. Her mother was in a bad way for the moment, physically. Why hadn't she thought of this? "I don't even know how my mom's finances are or her situation on help. I think she's been working alone, with just seasonal help. Her florist business hasn't ever been a huge moneymaker, but it's been a comfortable living if she does most of the work. I believe this collaboration with Rita and Tulip was to expand more." She let her words fade off as she thought about everything. "I can help out. I can fill in during the benefit. First, we have to find out how bad Mom is. If she's just unable to move around a lot…I know her—she'll sit on a stool and just do flower arrangements. If her hip is broken, it's a different story."

He nodded, looking grim. Then he shook his head. "Let's think positively, like your first scenario. Sprained ankle and a comfortable stool, with you filling in for her. Rita could probably get somebody else to do the flowers if she had to, but if you can get it done, that's a win for your mom and her business."

"You're right—" she said just as Austin came through the set of double doors. She set her coffee on the side table and stood, as well as Bret, who stepped closer to her. She was comforted by his presence.

Austin raked a hand through his short, dark hair and smiled warmly. "Good news. Nothing's broken. She does have a pretty banged up and bruised hip. She'll be sore but it's not broken and that's a good thing. She has strong bones. Her ankle is sprained but not as bad as it could be."

"Praise the Lord!" Relief engulfed Ellie and she smiled at Austin, then Bret.

Both men grinned.

"They're going to let her go home in a little while. We'll hang around and drive y'all back. How's that sound?"

"It sounds wonderful." She threw her arms around Austin. "Thank you. Thank you so much."

"I'm glad to help." Austin hugged her tightly before letting her go. "And that it wasn't as serious as it could have been."

She nodded as she stepped back and looked at Bret. She did not throw her arms around his neck. It didn't need to get any more awkward than it was. "And thank you for answering my call and bringing Austin. And for encouraging me this last hour." She was so very grateful he had answered her call.

"You're welcome." His gaze held hers. "And like we were talking about, this was the best scenario we could come up with. She may be able to work if she wants to. And you can help out. Here, have another donut." He picked up the abandoned bag and held it out to her.

She hadn't been able to look away from him and laughed in relief that her mother was not hurt worse and that he was making such an effort to help her through this. "Thank you for everything." She took a donut out of the large bag of donuts.

He took a donut and held one out to Austin.

Austin grinned, and took the donut and held it up. "Here's to a good prognosis."

She smiled, happy and refusing to let her confusion about Bret ruin her happiness about her mom. She held up her donut and Bret did too. Smiling, they all touched their donuts together and then they all took a bite.

* * *

By the time they checked her mom out of the hospital and had made it home, Ellie could not wait for Bret to say good-bye and head back to the ranch so she could breathe a sigh of relief, close herself up in her room, and try to make sense of her emotions.

She followed Austin and Bret down the hall as

Austin wheeled her mother down the hall to her bedroom. She tried not to think about how wide Bret's shoulders were, how narrow his hips were, and how muscled he was still.

"Thank you, boys, for coming to my rescue," her mother said as Austin and Bret helped her onto the bed. "I think I gave Ellie a heart attack when I fell. It was nice having you two show up so quickly."

"You're right, Mom. I very nearly did have a heart attack, so no more climbing on the ladder. Bret and Austin might not be near next time."

"Ellie is right," Austin said. "You need to stay off the ladder."

Feeling grateful, Ellie moved to the other side of the bed and helped get the pillows situated behind her mom.

"That's right, Ms. Betty," Bret agreed, quietly. "We all care about you."

A pillow Ellie was moving slid to the floor; Bret picked it up and handed it back to her. "Thank you," she said, her gaze riveted to his as she took the pillow from him.

"Anytime. Is there anything else we can do?" He let go of the pillow and stepped back. "I'd be a disaster arranging flowers but if you need me to lift or move things or deliver arrangements, you let me know. I'm not just a bull rider." He grinned at her mom.

Betty laughed cheerfully, and Ellie appreciated Bret's effort to lighten the moment.

"Thank you for the offer, Bret," her mom said. "That's really nice of you but tomorrow I'll sit on my cushioned stool with my leg propped on another stool while I do arrangements. Ellie will be my helper and will handle any task or problems I can't do." She looked at Ellie for confirmation. "You know, she's one of the most talented people who has ever worked with me. She just had bigger and better dreams to achieve."

Ellie felt uncomfortable with her mom's high praise. "Mom, you can count on me. I'll be right by your side tomorrow, and we will get the flowers done for the benefit. I'll do whatever you need me to do." She looked at Bret and then at Austin. "So, please, guys, don't worry. The flowers for the benefit will be ready. I will come out and make sure they're where they need to be. You'll be seeing more of me over the next couple of days than I had originally anticipated."

She knew Bret had been so very helpful but she couldn't tell whether hearing this bit of news would change things. She hoped that the animosity he'd shown toward her earlier wouldn't return. Right now, she didn't need the added pressure. She just needed her mother to get better.

Austin gave her an encouraging look. "We'll look forward to seeing you, and whatever we can do to help, we'll be there. Bret and I better get back to our duties. If you start hurting or need anything, please call me." He tipped his hat and then they walked out the door. "As a matter of fact you don't have a vehicle out here. If you give me a key we'll bring yours out here so yall have transportation."

"Oh thank you. I completely forgot." She went inside and grabbed her keys and took them back out to him.

He grinned. "I won't bother you when I bring the car back out. Just come out and get the keys. Take care. And don't forget to call if you need anything."

Ellie stared after them as they left. This had certainly been an odd day, especially considering they had started out so roughly, and now, she was supposed to call if she needed anything. She sighed. Then, hands on her hips, she smiled at her mom. "I guess we call if we need something."

Her mom's smile faltered. "I've really made a mess of things, haven't I? I know there is a lot of tension between you and Bret. You did handle yourself very well, though, and he and Austin were so good to me."

"Yes, they were. Don't you worry about me. I'm a big girl, and all I care about right now is helping you. And Bret showed that he cares too. So it will be all right. Might even be a good way for us to move on." She sat down easily on the bed beside her mom. "Mom, I will do whatever you need me to do. Please rest easy about that. We're going to make sure you get rave reviews over these decorations and that you get as busy as you're hoping for. I thought you'd be relaxing in your semi-retirement stage and here you are, trying to grow your business."

"But that's the thing. I'm not ready to retire, and this offer of teaming up with Rita and Tulip excites me." Excitement danced in her mother's eyes.

Ellie smiled. "I can see that. And Mom, I support whatever you want. There is nothing that dictates when you slow down…other than that ankle right now. But clearly, you aren't letting that slow you down."

"I'm going to take full advantage while you're here to help me out of this fix I've gotten myself into. I'm going to need your eyes and input out there on the ranch and then some help putting the arrangements together."

"Sure, whatever you need." She fought to keep her expression upbeat but inside it was hard as she realized that she would have to spend a good bit of time out at the ranch.

Would she be around Bret a lot?

Could she use the time to talk Bret into doing the interview? Even thinking the thought felt deceptive because she'd already resigned herself that the interview wouldn't happen. And considering he'd helped her mom today, she should honor his wishes. Right?

"I'll need you to take the mockups out there and make certain they're the right size for the areas that Rita is setting up for the various photo opportunities. I'm sure you can get Bret or Austin or somebody to help you hang them."

"Sure. Whatever you need, I'll do." And she would…and maybe Bret would reconsider and give her an interview.

CHAPTER FIVE

It was a beautiful September morning and Bret wasn't hurting as bad this morning as he had been. It usually took several days for his body, especially his shoulder, to recover. Lately, it was taking longer because of the injury he had sustained early in the year. He hadn't taken enough time off and hadn't given it time to heal completely. He was hoping this short window of time off would help.

He was unloading lumber from his truck for a pavilion they were building in the gardens that would simulate the backdrop for a wedding couple and the preacher, enabling guests interested in hiring Rita's services to take pictures and envision what a wedding would look like if designed by Rita, Tulip, and Betty.

It was a beautiful area closer to the river, which allowed the river to be a backdrop of the picture.

Cole was busy building everything his wife asked him to build, and Bret and his brothers were helping. This was not just a good cause to help with the new children's wing at the hospital but also to help these small businesses, and they were doing whatever they could to help.

Cole, who liked to build things, had been put in charge of making sure this pavilion, with its fancy archway, was perfect, along with all the other projects Rita had requested. He had people everywhere and as far as Bret could tell, things looked to be coming along nicely.

Though he didn't love building things like Cole did, Bret could handle a hammer and was as good at building any kind of fence, stall, or cattle pen a ranch might need. Their dad had taught them all how to ranch and one day Bret would have to give up bull riding and become a full-time rancher. He was mulling that over as he pulled the planks from his truck and stacked them. Levi had suggested he might consider running the new Montana ranch. The wild mustang program interested him, but the problem was his heart was here in the Texas Hill Country. Despite all of his traveling across the country competing, he took a piece of this ranch with him everywhere he went. This area was where he'd always assumed he'd retire to.

The Montana ranch was gorgeous, with sweeping vistas. Rita had taken amazing photographs of it when she, Levi, and her son Toby had visited. The problem was that he wasn't ready to give up bull riding. He was at the top of his game; if his shoulder could just hold out and heal up.

He set the wood down on the stack and then walked over to where Cole was working. "That's looking great. So where'd you get those old doors you're using there? They going to, like, just stay open and then they're going to walk through them?"

"I got these from that old barn we have over in the south pasture."

"The one that was half fallen down?"

"That's the one."

"We probably should have restored that place."

"I agree. It's too far gone to restore now but these old doors were salvageable. When I showed them to Tulip and Rita, they about went crazy." He grinned over at Levi as his brother came striding up. "Didn't our wives go crazy over these doors?"

"Never thought two old doors could get that kind of reaction out of one woman, much less two. Shows what I know. Women still remain a mystery to me."

They all laughed at that. Bret had to agree with his brothers as his thoughts shifted instantly to Ellie.

"Anybody have a report on Ms. Betty today?" Levi asked. "I've got to run up to the house in a minute and get Toby when he wakes up from his nap. I'm going to drive over to Fredericksburg and get him a new outfit for the benefit. That kid loves Western clothes and since Rita is swamped, I told her I'd do it. I thought I'd take him by to see her. She's a nice lady and adores him. I thought it might cheer her up."

"That's a great idea," Cole said. "Tulip talked to Ellie and said she's upbeat and determined to put on a happy face but she's hurting. A visit by Toby would probably do her some good."

"Then we'll swing by there. That little boy can brighten anyone's day."

Levi's adoration was clear and Bret grinned. "You make a good daddy, I think."

"I love it and can't wait to have a baby with Rita. I'm hoping to adopt Toby but it's a delicate situation with his dad having died here. I might not be able to, and it just depends on what he wants in the end. But I love him like he was my own. Bret, you're missing out. Marriage and family is the best thing that's ever happened to me. It's going to be your turn one day."

Cole laughed. "You, Austin, and Jake are missing out." He pointed his hammer at Bret. "How's it been since seeing Ellie?"

Bret scowled. "It's been awkward. But then, with her mom hurting herself, and me and Austin going to help her—well, that added another dimension to it. Austin did great helping her out and more than likely called to check on her this morning. We can ask him when he gets here."

Cole shook his head. "He had an emergency and won't be here. That guy has too many emergencies."

"But he was supposed to be off."

Cole hitched a shoulder. "One of his patients who he admitted in the emergency room a couple of nights ago took a turn for the worse, and he went to check on the older man."

Bret admired his brother. He had energy; the passion he had for saving lives and taking care of people just kept him going. Bret wondered sometimes how he did it. "Well, one day when Austin decides to get married, whoever he marries is going to have to get used to a really strange schedule."

Levi shook his head. "Like you."

"Right. Well, I guess if you're doing something you love, you don't really notice how busy it is. Jake will have to be the next in line to marry because I think me and Austin aren't ready."

"Jake is going to go down fighting." Cole nodded toward the round pen near the barns, where Jake was inside, working a horse. "That fella has his mind on having a good time building his ranch."

"Then I guess the next Tanner brother to fall will be a surprise." Bret reached for another plank, ready for the conversation to be over. His mind had switched over to Ellie and what could have been. And he didn't want to think about that anymore. But it seemed since she'd shown up that she was on his mind no matter how hard he tried to block her.

He didn't need his brothers realizing that, though. After unloading the rest of the planks, he drove his truck back to the parking area to get it out of the way. He was just getting out of the truck when he saw Ellie drive up and park. He hung his head. This was torture. But there was no hiding from it right now. With steps that felt as if concrete had been poured into his boots, he headed her way.

* * *

"Can I help you carry that?"

Ellie was pulling the huge arrangement from the back of the florist van. She had hoped not to run into him and of course, as her luck would have it, he was the first one she ran into. Although she wanted to be around him so maybe she could get this stinking interview, she was hesitant about being around him. She couldn't have it both ways and she knew it.

"Thanks. That would be very helpful. One thing about my mom—she can make Texas-sized flower arrangements. And that humongous cow head stuffed in the middle of all that dry flower arrangement is heavy."

He gave a nod and looked at it skeptically. "I've got to say, I never thought I'd see a cow head in the middle of dried flowers."

"Well, believe me, when it gets put above that entrance that she told me was being built for people to walk through to the pavilion, it will be gorgeous. I need to have you and some others help me hold that above the door where it's going to hang so I can photograph it and then take it back to my mom so she'll know how many of the real flowers to put in it to balance it out and make it absolutely gorgeous. Believe me, she and Rita are going to have an amazing setup here for future business. While also helping make this place beautiful for the charity."

"Yeah, they're working hard and have half the

town here working. There's people everywhere. And Cole is working on the doors you're looking for. He got them from a real old barn that we have out here that was falling down."

"That's awesome. Mom described what she thought they were going to look like but she hasn't seen it and neither have I."

"Well, come with me and I'll take you to it."

They walked beside each other across the pasture, and when she saw the doors, a huge smile spread across her face. "That's so old but perfect. And by the time we get the flowers up and the lanterns set around it…oh goodness, it's going to be a great entrance. And the thing about it is it's going to be just as beautiful for a wedding as it will be for a party or charity event like this, or any gathering. So it's going to be great—just what they were hoping for."

"Alrighty then. Let me set this here on this workbench." He set it down on a bench very easily and then looked around. "I have to find a ladder and probably somebody to help me. You need it up there, right?" He pointed to a bar with a hook on it above the doors.

"I sure do."

"Then I'll be right back."

While he walked away, she watched him go and all the nerves she had been feeling rattled around inside her as he strode away with that swagger that he had always had. It was bred into him, she thought. He had always had it but when he rode a bull, after he finished his eight-second ride and dismounted,Bret Tanner was a little bit cocky and the crowd loved it. He would use that swagger and walk there in the middle of that arena and throw his hat up, salute everybody and then he'd do a bow. And then he'd sometimes have to run out of that pen and dive for the railings to get out of the way of the bull that was still in the pen when he was doing all that stuff.

It used to drive her crazy and scare her to death. But he'd always been quick on his feet. He was so agile, so…perfect. There was no denying it; the man was still every bit the heartthrob he had always been. And she knew this was going to be as tough as she thought it would be.

Her mouth was dry; she turned away and looked straight at Levi.

"Hey there, Ellie. How's your mom?"

"She's going to make it. Thanks to your brothers getting there to help me to get her to the hospital."

He grinned and nodded in the direction of Bret. She didn't even have to look over her shoulder to know who he was nodding at. "My brother there—you know, you two have unfinished business, don't you think?"

She crossed her arms and stared right back at Levi. "Now why would you say that? I have been happy with my life in Houston. And he's obviously really happy with his life. So, I'm not sure what you mean about unfinished business."

"About whatever happened between y'all. I have a feeling you felt neglected, and rightly so. And in order to save your own heart, you broke it off."

How in the world could Levi Tanner read her mind? "You think that?"

"Yes, I do. And you know me, being the younger brother and pretty centered on my own rebellion back in those days against all the papa-rats that were coming around here. You know the papa-rats—as I like to call the jerks who chased me around all those years, trying to take my picture and say bad things about me in the tabloids. Anyway, I had my suspicions, but I didn't exactly think anybody needed to be getting married back then. But, I wanted to tell you, I don't think Bret's ever gotten over you."

Her heart thudded against her rib cage like somebody was using a jackhammer inside her ribs, trying to get out. "Levi, why are you telling me all this?"

"Isn't it obvious? I think you two need to try again. I see you don't have a ring on your finger. Your mama and my mama are good buddies, and Ms. Betty never said anything about you getting married. And honest to goodness, I've never heard any rumors about you having some great love of your life since you've been living in Houston. You keep to yourself while you're in town just so you don't run into Bret."

Unease filled her. Levi had some kind of magic ball he was obviously looking into. "Levi, Bret and I went our separate ways years ago. I live in Houston and your brother has his own life. And as far as I can tell, not one single thing has changed about our situation. I am not going to wait around on him to finally decide that I'm important to him." *Oh drats, she hadn't meant to say that!*

Levi grinned knowingly. "I knew I was right. You got tired of being second in his life. You got tired of the tabloid stories. I have a feeling you don't realize how bad you hurt him."

She wanted to ask him about all the women in the tabloids that Bret denied was anything, but she didn't; she kept that to herself. She never thought she'd say it, but she saw Bret coming back their way and she was relieved. "Look, he's coming back. I'm telling you, don't start this stuff because it's not going to make him happy. He is not happy with me being around."

"All the more reason for you to be here. The man does seem a little too riled up about you being involved in this than he should be. I think if he was over you, he wouldn't really care if you were here or not. But he cares."

She didn't know what to say to that but didn't have to react because Bret reached them. He was carrying a ladder.

"Hey Levi, since you're just standing around yapping, you can help me hang this floral arrangement. Ellie needs to take a picture for her mom before heading back to town."

"Why, big brother, I didn't think you ever needed your little brother's help."

Bret frowned at Levi's joking around—it was a *don't-start-that-junk* look.

Ellie remembered many such looks passing between the brothers back in high school. She was an only child and had missed the sibling dynamic, but smiled now because she'd always enjoyed watching the brothers' interactions.

"Hold this." Bret picked up the decorated cow skull from the workbench and placed it in Levi's hands. "I'll climb up on the ladder and you hold it up."

"Sure. Don't fall off that ladder, though. A guy like you probably doesn't have any balance."

She laughed, knowing he was teasing Bret because if there was one thing a bull rider had, it was excellent balance. You didn't stay on a crazy bucking bull's back for eight seconds without it.

"Funny," Bret said.

Levi winked at her. "I'm getting to him."

She couldn't help laughing.

Moments later, with Bret on the ladder holding the flower arrangement in place and with Levi supporting it from beneath, she snapped a photo for her mom.

Bret looked over his shoulder at her, and she snapped another shot, catching him looking directly into the camera. She snapped another photo—just in case she didn't get a good one the first time. Not that her mother needed a picture of Bret.

"Okay, I have what I need," she said, reluctant to let this moment go.

Levi tipped his hat. "I'll go see what else Rita has for me to do. Good to see you, Ellie."

"Thanks. You as well," she said and watched him leave.

Bret climbed off the ladder. "I can take it back to the car for you."

"Thanks, but I can take it." She reached for it, but he held on.

"I don't mind. It's heavy." His gaze seemed to search hers.

She felt breathless and unnerved, and let go. "Okay." Needing space, she stepped back and started walking. He fell into step beside her. They hadn't spoken in years and now here they were, spending time together. And she felt more vulnerable than she'd like to admit, walking next to him. It took her back to memories she knew were better left in the dark recesses of her memory.

"What are you thinking about?" he asked, startling her from her thoughts.

They'd reached the car and she bit her lip, hoping her thoughts weren't showing in her eyes. "Just thinking about how beautiful this is going to be."

He stared from beneath the dip of his hat brim. "Never took you for a liar."

A liar? "And there's a lot of things I never took you for. Turned out I was wrong," she snapped before she could get a grip on the anger his words had set off inside her. *He'd* been the liar.

They stared at each other. The tension of yesterday's meeting by the river was back between them. After what he'd done for her mother, she felt guilt now but the anger she'd felt for so long at being shoved to the sidelines of his life after he'd asked her to wait for him. He'd gotten it started and won a championship and had been well on his way to a second one when she'd realized she'd never be the main focus of his life. It still hurt after all this time, knowing that he'd always had her on a back shelf and it had taken her so long to realize it. Even when the tabloids had shown her the truth over and over again.

"I know you would much rather I wasn't here, but I am. And now, with my mom's injury, I'll be here longer than planned. But I'm sure you won't be, so we should be able to make these next few days work. Just don't call me a liar. You're the one who is not going to give me an interview. But just because I needed an interview from you doesn't mean I'm going to take any attitude from you."

"Wow, the Ellie I remember didn't have this hardcore side to her."

She scowled, disgusted. "Oh yeah? Well, maybe

the Ellie you once knew got tired of people walking all over her. See you later, Bret. Thanks for helping me." With that, she closed the door to the van, then opened the driver's door and climbed inside. Thankfully, he didn't try to stop her. She had said too much. She didn't have a poker face, and she had shown all her cards. It wasn't exactly how she planned it. Then again, nothing about this trip was how she planned it.

CHAPTER SIX

Bret watched Ellie drive away and felt a huge sense of loss watching her go. He had halfway been teasing her with the comment about lying, and she'd taken it to heart. He knew exactly how she felt now. She felt as if he had lied to her when he'd been rodeoing, and he hadn't.

He'd told her over and over that the stories about him were not true.

"That didn't look like it went so well." Jake came up beside him.

He slid his brother a sidelong glance. "Not at all. I don't know why I thought after yesterday that we could at least get on speaking terms again."

"Why can't you?"

"She just came here to get an interview from me and I'm not giving it to her. Then her mom had her accident, and Ellie called me to help. But it turns out despite it being my phone she called to get the help for her mom that her opinion of me is still in the tank."

"Change her opinion."

"I'm not sure I want to."

"Sure you do," Jake encouraged, his voice trailing off as a truck with the True Love, Texas Veterinarian Clinic logo pulled into the parking area and parked across from them.

Bret shot his brother a glance as a perky brunette hopped from the cab. Jake stared; his jaw had a pulse to it and Bret knew he was gritting his teeth, something he did when he was stressed. *Interesting.* She had on a ball cap and an oxford shirt with a logo over her heart. She paused when she saw them.

* * *

The day after she had spoken to Bret so rudely, she came downstairs to find her mother hobbling around in the kitchen on crutches. She had the coffee carafe in her hand as she tried to maneuver back to the coffeemaker without spilling the water out of it.

"Mom, hang on. I'll do that. What are you doing?"

Her mother turned toward her, looking frustrated as water splashed out of the precariously held carafe. "I'm trying to make coffee. This is so aggravating."

Betty Seton was an independent woman. Ellie knew this was hard on her. "Mom, it's okay. Here, sit down on a barstool and let me help you." She took the carafe and waited as her mom sank onto the barstool with an exaggerated sigh.

"Fine. Thanks."

"It's not going to be too much longer, and you'll be able to toss those crutches. But you just need to be a little more patient."

"I'm tired of sitting on the barstool, watching you rush around, bringing me supplies."

Her upbeat mom sounded really frustrated. "It's fine, Mom. I don't mind getting supplies for you. But today is your lucky day because you won't have to watch me run around getting things for you because I'm heading out to the flower farm, remember? I'll be out of your hair for a little while. And then, together, we will get this done. It's going to be okay."

Betty dropped her head to her hand. "You're right. I'm just not used to others doing everything for me. I don't like it. I used to drive your father crazy."

Ellie smiled at the memory, because it was so true. She finished making the coffee, and when it was done she filled a mug and set it beside her mom. "But he loved you anyway, despite all of your independent ways."

"Yes, he did." She looked up and gave a rueful smile. "And I'm not easy to love. I am fairly set in my ways and demanding and nosy."

"And can get really uptight when you're anxious," Ellie added, her heart tugging.

"Yes, really anxious." Her mother cocked her head to the side.

Ellie filled her own cup with coffee and leaned against the counter. "Don't look at me like that, Mom."

"You know I'm going to say you're exactly like me, and yesterday, when you returned from the Tanner ranch, I could tell you were wound extremely tight."

"No, I'm fine."

"You can't lie to me, young lady. Want to talk about it?"

Never took you for a liar. Bret's words echoed through her. She had overreacted and she knew it. She was just so sensitive about their past. She set her coffee down and paced to the window. She stared out and tried to monitor her words but gave up. She spun to her mom. "It is so frustrating seeing him. I would try to hide it, but I can't."

"Why don't you try to make up with him? Barbara and I have hopes that now that you are older, you two will make up. We both agree that neither of you have ever been the same since the breakup. It seems something is missing out of both of your lives. You've both needed some time to focus on your careers."

"With him, it never changes. His career and dating seem to go hand-in-hand."

"And you know this how?"

She closed her eyes for a moment, not believing she had said that. Then she looked at her mom. "I follow him on social media and read about him in the tabloids occasionally. But I'm in the entertainment news cycle and staying informed is part of my job," she said weakly, knowing by the pitying look her mom had leveled on her that she didn't believe Ellie for one minute. "Okay—I can't help it. He hurt me and I can't forget or let it go. It's pathetic. I mean, really, I look him up on social media and read the tabloids just to see if he's in there." She was pathetic. And she hated it. "But it's part of my job," she repeated, realizing she'd said too much.

Her mom's expression softened, and her eyes mellowed with sympathy. "Are you sure it's that much part of your job?"

Tears strained for release and she blinked them back. "I'm personally interested but right now it's definitely part of my job. It's…it's actually imperative that I get this interview with him. If not, you may have a house guest longer than you planned."

"Are you saying you'll lose your job?"

She nodded. "That's exactly what I'm saying. My boss gave me that assignment once he found out that I knew Bret personally. Our rankings are struggling, and he needs to get them up, or they have to do major cuts and I'm at the top of the list."

"But that's so unfair. Why would you be at the top of the list?"

"He doesn't value entertainment news as important as other news. To be honest, I'm really starting to lose interest anyway. I've come to terms with that admitting it."

"If you're losing interest, you're talented enough to find something different. You know, I'd love for you to join me in the business. And I'm thanking you so much for helping me now. I'm going to need extra help if I start getting more business."

"Thank you for the offer, Mom, but I just don't think I could move back here permanently. One day, Bret will move back here and I can't run into him all the time. Or avoid him all the time." It was hard enough dealing with her feelings for him from a distance. Seeing him the last few days only proved her greatest fear—that she might not ever get over him.

Her mother reached out and gently squeezed her hand. "Maybe this time, while you're here, you'll concentrate on fixing this rift. It would be the best thing for both of you. Clear the air, get everything out in the open. And either you'll get back together or you'll at least move forward. And then maybe you can figure out what you want to do with the rest of your life."

Her mother's words wrapped around her heart as truth—if she could come to terms with how their relationship, their love had ended, then maybe she could move on and maybe even find someone new to love. Because it was obvious there would never be anything between her and Bret.

"I can see your mind working. I want the best for you."

She smiled at her mom. "You've given me good advice. I was just sitting here, thinking about all the time I wasted on all my thoughts that had to do with Bret—good, bad, worried…all of them. I need to just get it out in the open and get it over with and let it go."

"Exactly. Everything will be better if you do that."

She took a deep breath. "I hope so, but I really doubt it."

CHAPTER SEVEN

Bret had come into town for lunch when he spotted what looked like the florist van on the side of the road. *What was wrong now?* Pulling in behind the van, he got out and saw that it had a flat. He walked around to the side and spotted Ellie walking around, talking on the phone. When she spotted him, she said something into the phone and then hung up.

"You look like you're having a problem."

She did not look happy to see him. He had thought about her all night and had been distracted this morning as he had been out riding horses with Jake. His brother had noticed his distraction. Everybody was noticing his distraction. He needed to figure out what was going on between him and Ellie. Needed to get it out and get it over with, just like his brothers had told him.

"I have a flat. And I called someone to come and haul this van in because my mom does not have a spare tire in it. I don't want to call her because she has enough stress on her already."

"That's not good. So someone's coming to get it? Were you going somewhere?"

"I was going to a flower farm we buy from to pick up the flowers so we could get them back this evening and start working on the arrangements for the benefit."

"Don't they deliver?"

"Normally, but Mom uses a small wholesaler on the outskirts of San Antonio, and they are shorthanded right now and no one can deliver, so I'm going to pick them up. Mom's holding down the fort. She's doing okay, moving around on her crutches some, but I still need to get them and get back. This has already put me back thirty minutes and it's going to take me at least three hours to get there and get back—maybe even longer."

"Do you think if we put them in my truck, we'll

have plenty of room in the backseat?"

"They'll be in boxes, so we can stack them if we need to, but I can't ask you to do that."

"You can't ask me, or you don't want to ask me?"

Her brow knit and she frowned. "Okay, I don't want to ask you."

"This is ridiculous." He raked a hand through his hair, staring at her from beneath the rim of his Stetson. "We've got to get over this. We have a past that we're not happy with, but we need to let it go and we both know it."

She crossed her arms. "So is your offer to help me contingent on whether I make an apology or a concession for the last meeting that we had?"

He removed his hat and slapped it on the side of his leg. The woman frustrated him. "No, you don't have to do any of that. I'm just saying we need to get this out."

She walked around to the driver's side of the van, reached inside and came out with her purse. "Maybe we do but I just need a ride at the moment."

She stomped past him, yanked open the passenger

side door and got inside his truck.

He shook his head, and then went around and slid behind the steering wheel. He shot her a grudging look. "You always did have a temper, and it doesn't look good on you right now."

She turned to look at him. "Is that right? Well, I haven't thought that the tabloid pictures of you all these years with one woman after another on your arm has looked very good on you either."

He gritted his teeth. "So we are right back to that. How many times do I have to tell you not to believe what you see in those gossip rags? You have this media-based, fake, contorted view of me. I apologized to you years ago and told you then that all those women you see me with in the tabloids are not what you thought."

"Right. I don't know why I even said that. It no longer matters anyway."

* * *

The miles ticked by as Bret stared straight ahead and

drove. How had so much happened between them, leaving them at this point in their relationship that they had become complete and total strangers? It was hard to imagine because they once were so close. He focused back on the road. His hands tightened on the steering wheel.

She stared straight ahead and hadn't said much in the last five miles they had traveled.

"Is this how it's going to be all the way to this place we're going? Twenty miles of the cold shoulder?"

"Honestly, Bret, I'm just not sure what to talk about."

"I totally understand," he said. "Last person I expected to walk into Manny's the other night was you. Then, with your question…"

She turned slightly in the truck so that she was turned toward him better. "I can assure you the last thing I wanted to do was come and ask you for an interview. It was a last resort. But don't worry, I don't need an interview with you anymore. I should have told my boss no the moment he suggested or demanded that I get this interview. There is no way that I would have done it, if I had another option. And I realize now that I do have an option—it's just to stand up to my boss and say I'm not getting an interview from Bret Tanner, so fire me. I'll go ahead and find me another job. And that's what I'm going to do."

He pressed the brake and shot her a glance. "You're going to lose your job?"

"Yes. I told you I wouldn't have asked if I hadn't been desperate."

He tightened his grip on the steering wheel as acid churned in his gut and his mind turned her words over and over. He felt bad for her but… "Look, we have a past that's not been pretty. A past that I never completely understood. And I'm not going to sit down with you and discuss my life in an interview with the person who turned my world completely upside down." Anger rose up in his chest.

She laughed harshly. "You think I turned your life upside down?"

"You did. You told me you would wait for me and then you moved on. You changed your mind. And you broke it off and started college. You blindsided me."

Her face was red, and her eyes flashed when he looked at her. *So be it. What was new?*

"You made the tabloids every other day," she fumed. "Sometimes, every day. You were rumored to be having affairs with all kinds of women. And you expected me to believe none of that was true? But aside from that, you never put me in the number-one position. I was always waiting, always left behind. And, to be honest, when you asked me to wait for you, I didn't tell you what I really thought and wanted. You broke my heart. That's it—you broke my heart. There, now you know. And I never recovered from that."

"I broke your heart? I had made plans. But it's no big deal. It's in the past."

She stared at him. "What plans had you made? You never talked to me about any plans. You never acted as if we were going anywhere. You just were so focused on the rodeo—I was just left out in the cold while you were on the front of all those tabloids. So did you never stop to think about me, how I felt?"

He pulled the truck over onto the side of the road.

Traffic was whizzing by because I-35 was very busy and he still had one exit to go before they could get off it and get into less traffic. But he had to be looking at her. "I had told you over and over again that those rumors and photos were all staged. Those were cowgirls in the NFR. We talk. Don't you have regular conversations with people? I couldn't even say hello without a photo being taken of me and my picture being splashed across the tabloids the next day. I couldn't help it if it looked like I was having an affair. I got tired of it and then you got to where you were just distrusting me all the time. It was tiring. And frustrating. But I thought we worked through it and I still had plans for us. I thought if I could just win the NFR, then the stress would be off me. And maybe we could—"

"Let's just stop talking about it. It's over. And I want it to be that way. Completely."

She stared at him with hurt in her eyes and he felt for her. And suddenly he questioned whether maybe some of what she said was true. *Had he just expected too much of her?* Just because he knew the tabloids were lying about him over and over again? Had he expected her—just because she loved him—to believe his word when she had to see the lies over and over again?

"So you just gave up on us and decided to go get your degree in journalism and moved on."

"Yes," she said tightly.

"And you've been okay?" He suddenly wanted to know. Something he had never asked her because they hadn't seen each other. He had never asked his mom, either.

"I've been successful, to a point. Nothing to write home about or be hugely ecstatic about. I need to go and pick up these flowers. This conversation is pointless. We are completely at odds with each other. You have your story, and I have my story."

His heart squeezed, seeing the chasm between them growing. A small portion of him didn't want it to get any wider. "Look, what if we tried just to move on? Just decide here and now to get past the hurt that we each feel over what happened between us. I'm willing to do it. I'm sorry how it ended. I know it's too late for us, but I don't want us to go on forever like this. Our moms are best friends. For them, we need to get over this."

"Fine. Can we do it?" Her gaze challenged him, and from the set of her mouth, he knew she didn't think they could.

"I truly believe that you and I can do anything we set our minds to. At least, we used to believe that."

"That was a long time ago."

"I still believe it. If we want it."

She looked away and stared out the window.

His fingers suddenly ached to trace the line of her jaw.

"Let's try. It won't be easy—you know that. You just don't forgive and forget and go on like nothing ever happened."

"Why not? I'm planning on doing it. When I make my mind to get on the bull and ride it, I don't get on it thinking I'm going to *try* to ride it. I get on with the plan to ride the full eight seconds."

"Where your career is concerned, you always did have that attitude."

Her words hit their mark. "Right. When I get on that bull, my mind is focused on the one thing I'm going to do, and that's to ride that bull. No looking back. If I get on that bull with any less of a mindset, then I have regrets and I don't often have regrets in my bull riding career. But, Ellie, I have a lot of regrets where we're concerned. I guess if you hadn't shown up this weekend, it would have kept on that way. But I'm tired of it. I'm really tired of it and I want to ride this bull. I want to be successful in making you and me at least have a friendship to where we can see each other on the street and not try to run the other way. Or you can come home to visit your mom and not be afraid to go to Manny's and eat a chicken fried steak. Because I know how much you love a chicken fried steak. And Manny still makes the best in Texas."

She smiled, her eyes a little bit misty. "Okay. I always remembered how you could set your mind on something and how you could go for it. It was one of the things I loved about you."

It hit him in that moment that maybe that was how he was in his life, but had he had that attitude about the two of them back then? Or had he had his mind so set on conquering the bull-riding championships that she was right—that he had put her on the back burner and just expected her to wait and be satisfied with being second in his life? He was sorry about that. But they couldn't go through that again and they couldn't move forward on that. They could move forward on regaining a friendship. But that's all it could be—a friendship. They truly did have too much water under the bridge, too much of a past to try for a relationship again.

But at least being friends was where they had to go first before doing anything else.

CHAPTER EIGHT

They arrived at the flower farm, and Ellie could not believe the conversation she and Bret had had on the drive there.

Were they both at fault for what had happened? Should she have trusted him? She thought back to all the things she had endured, the articles, and she knew that it would have taken someone much stronger than her to have not doubted Bret. For one, just seeing the beautiful women in the photos was hard on her because she knew she didn't compare. And it made her feel inferior and put her in a place that wasn't good for her. She questioned a lot of things about herself at that time—her looks, her ability to hold her man—and his love of her.

So many things had poisoned her thoughts during that time. If she'd been more sure of herself, could she have believed him when he'd swore the tabloids were lying?

She got out of the truck, glad for a chance to step away from the conversation. Caroline, of Caroline's Flowers, waved and came to greet them.

"There you are." She threw her arms around Ellie. "When your mama called me and told me you were in town and coming to pick up these flowers, I was so excited. How long has it been since I've seen you? Three, maybe four years? I've lost track." Holding her by each arm, Caroline stepped back and surveyed Ellie. "You look real good. We've missed you."

"I've missed you, too, Caroline. It's so good to see you."

Caroline smiled. "And you're Bret Tanner. I remember you, too. I know your mom and your dad. How are you doing? You're the bull rider, right? I think you've been burning it up on those bulls. You going to do good at the NFR this year?"

"I hope so. I'm going to give it my all."

"Don't you have a shoulder that's giving you a bunch of trouble?"

"Yes, ma'am. I see you weren't telling a story—you really do see some news."

"I don't fib about nothing. I was watching the night you got stomped by that bull and I was thinking, oh my word, we're fixing to lose one of our own on national TV. It was terrible. It's taken a little while to get over it, too, hasn't it? I mean, you've been riding but you haven't been riding those bulls like you normally do."

"Yes, ma'am. It's taking me a little while but I'm doing better. My shoulder is better and I'm feeling much stronger. I'm riding enough to keep my points up, thank you very much, and I've been doing, you know, training for it."

"Well, now, that's great. So you brought Ellie out here to get our flowers for the charity and we want to thank you for being involved in this event, Bret. We want to raise money for this new hospital wing and having your family and you involved—the kids are really going to enjoy that. So we thank you. Now, y'all come on in here and get these flowers. I know you and your mama are going to have a lot of work to do making these arrangements."

They followed her inside. Beautiful assortments of lilies and roses filled several buckets.

"Those are gorgeous. Here, I think we can get all of those in the backseat of my truck."

"You can. They're all piled in really well. I made sure and got enough of them in the buckets so there weren't too many. The van works better but this will do. They'll do fine. You just have to keep it cool in there on the drive back."

"We can do that." Ellie smiled at him. He was a nice guy. Always had been; still was. Her heart clenched a little with wishful thinking about what could have been between them, and she knew he was probably right. They had been young—too young. Maybe if they had just had a better chance, with age they could have made it.

They loaded up the flowers and then waved good-bye to Caroline. She told them she would see them at the charity, and then they headed back to True Love.

"So how is your shoulder?"

"It's good. Now, whether I'm really the one to beat at the NFR this year in December, I'm not sure. Reputation has a lot to do with that, sometimes. And points. I've been hanging on but I can't promise you I'm going to come out the winner. I've been giving it everything I have."

They drove for a little bit.

"Ellie, I've been thinking about it since we talked more and you might have been right. I might not have given you the place in my life you deserved. Maybe— no, not maybe—I give everything in my life my all. But when I rode out of here to start making my way in the NFR, that's what I had planned. In my brain, I was telling myself that I was doing it for us. For you and me. I'd get my reputation and I'd be the best, and we would start our life together. But you did have to go through a lot." He looked at her and she saw pain in his eyes and then he looked away.

Her heart clenched tighter. She took a deep breath. Hearing him say those words really hit home.

"Bret, I was thinking, too. And maybe you were

right—we were both too young."

He glanced at her again. "No, I was too young—I expected too much from you. But the reality is I didn't give you what you were due, and that was my full attention if you were going to be my wife eventually. I didn't let you know that with my actions."

"Then maybe we just weren't meant to be."

They traveled again for a little while and he sighed. "Maybe you're right. But I just want you to know I'm sorry."

She looked out the window and she knew that he was nowhere near as sorry as she was.

CHAPTER NINE

Standing in the yard of the Tanner ranch, Ellie gazed around at the beautiful gardens, the pavilion, and the different floral arrangements that she and her mother had finished for the event. Her mother was very happy with how it had all turned out, as were Rita and Tulip.

Ellie was happy too.

She was actually so glad she had come home. It was so strange. She was fairly certain Bret wasn't changing his mind about the interview, so she had probably lost her job…but she may have re-established her friendship with Bret.

The possibility of mending the hole that was in her heart was a relief. Was needed.

While they'd worked on the arrangements yesterday, Ellie had discussed her and Bret's conversation with her mother, and Betty had been extremely excited. "Putting things in perspective is important," her mother had said. "It sometimes takes time to realize the problems that arise between two people in a relationship."

It was so true, Ellie thought, as she put the finishing touches on the arrangements before the guests started to arrive. Her mother sat at the promotion table, ready to take all the orders and to talk to anyone who had questions about the flowers. There would be good food, dancing, and a lot of networking done tonight. And a lot of money changing hands as donations came in.

"It's looking awesome, Ellie." Rita came over and gave Ellie a hug. "You and Betty did an amazing job. The photos of the guests in front of the arrangements are going to be gorgeous. I'll be busy all evening, taking photos of couples who are donating to the hospital wing. I'm certain we'll get a lot of business from donating our time and talents to help the charity raise the needed money."

"I think so too. I really enjoyed helping, and Mom loved it. She is so talented. I'm glad to see more people being exposed to her work."

Rita nudged her elbow. "Yes, she is very talented, but you are too."

"I can make flower arrangements, but my mother is the creative genius behind all this. She has the vision, which is something I've never had."

"Maybe you are short-changing yourself and rely on Betty's creativity instead of seeking your own. Your own vision might be something completely different and unique."

Ellie thought about that. "I might try it. But I'm a reporter."

"I think we're all a little variation of different things. I'm a photographer, a mother, a wedding planner now also. I think you're more than you're giving yourself credit for, although being able to write an article is an amazing feat to me. I know I could never do that. But I'm going to try doing a few articles on my blog. I might ask for some help."

"I'd be glad to help if you need it."

"Great. I heard Bret rescued you off the side of the road and carried you to pick up the flowers. How's it going with you two?"

"It actually went fine. We're going to work on becoming friends again."

"Friends?" Rita stared at her. "I wouldn't give up on loving him."

"No, not going there. We're doing good to take this step of being around each other." It was so true. She and Bret getting back together wasn't something she was ready to think about—she was actually a little scared of the idea.

* * *

Bret looked up from where he was signing bull-riding photos for children at the cancer center. He would take them tomorrow and hand them out and talk to the children as part of the program he was starting to benefit children with cancer. His good friend, one of the bull riders who had ridden and competed against him for years, had recently had a son who had gone through cancer. Bret had helped out as much as he could, in any way he could, as he had watched his friend and his family and his child go through what Bret prayed no family would ever have to go through again. He knew that families would have to continue to suffer through this horrible disease, but he had vowed that he would do whatever he could to help find a cure, especially for children. Thankfully, the use of immunology treatments combined with his other treatment plan had worked: his friend's son was cancer-free.

Thinking about the emotions that they had all gone through when that little Jeremiah had been able to ring that bell and proclaim he was cancer-free had been amazing. Bret had been quietly making trips into the children's wings of hospitals for the last year. He'd deliver signed autograph photos but mostly he'd talk to the kids, or listen, or do puzzles with them. Whatever they wanted. He wasn't looking for any notoriety, but when he'd realized he could help raise money for the hospital wing, he'd gladly agreed to help at this benefit, hoping that his name, in some small way, could help bring in more money.

Jeremiah and his family were the guests of honor tonight. They were going to tell his story and hope to help raise money too. When Jeremiah walked into the gathering, Bret was waiting. The little boy was about the age of Levi's stepson Toby. And he was decked out in cowboy attire just as much as Toby was. He spotted Bret and waved, then came running. Jason and Jill, Jeremiah's mom and dad, followed him, both of them smiling broadly.

"Bret! Bret!" Jeremiah threw himself into Bret's arms.

Bret closed his eyes and held onto the kid. He was Jeremiah's godfather and he hoped one day he would have his own kids. But he had to find a wife before that could happen. "Hey, little fella. I'm so glad you made it. And aren't you looking spiffy in your fancy getup there? I like that shirt. And are those new boots?"

Jeremiah looked up at him and grinned, nodding his head. "They are. Daddy took me and we got me some new ones. Do you like my buckle?"

"I do like it. Every cowboy needs a big shiny buckle. It's as big as a hub cap."

He cocked his head to the side. "What's a hub cap?"

Bret smiled. "You know, on your daddy's truck—that thing in the middle of the tire."

"The shiny round thing." Jeremiah looked skeptically at his buckle. "It's not that big. Daddy's wheels on his truck are almost bigger than me. Me and Mama have a hard time getting in his truck."

"You're right. I'm just teasing you about the buckle. Maybe your dad needs a smaller truck if you and your mama can't climb in there. It is a big truck." He hitched a teasing brow at Jason.

Both Jill and Jason laughed.

Jill smiled at him and then up at Jason. "He's definitely going to have to do that since we just found out we're having another baby."

Jason grinned at him, and Bret's mouth fell open. "Congratulations. That is amazing. I'm happy for y'all. Buddy, you are definitely going to need a lower-to-the-ground truck. No way Jill's going to be able to climb up into that tall one."

"We're going shopping pretty quick because as

hard as it is to believe, I like these little kiddos in my life much more than I like those big wheels on my truck."

"I'm glad you do, Daddy, 'cause I like you best too." Jeremiah beamed up at his dad.

Bret's heart cinched with gratefulness for his friends and this adorable little boy.

Jason put his arm around Jill and looked around. "And we love you best. Bret, looks like a lot of people came out for this."

Bret smiled at him. "Yes, they did. We're going to build that new cancer wing for the hospital. Everyone is excited."

"That's awesome. We can't thank you enough for that."

Bret set Jeremiah on the ground and stood up. "Come on. My mom and dad want to say hello, and then we can get you some food." He took Jeremiah's hand and then they all walked toward his mom and dad, who stood beside the center fountain in the rose garden area. As he crossed the grounds, he spotted Ellie.

She was watching him and his gut tightened as their eyes collided. He could see questions in her eyes, and he figured she was probably starting to catch on that this benefit might be more personal to him than he had let on. Especially after the flowers had been made up and little Jeremiah's picture had been on it, with his story. And that of his family. And how the bull-riding community had come together behind them as Jason had been without insurance when Jeremiah had been diagnosed with cancer.

His parents, Barbara and Daniel, had met Jeremiah and his family before they had donated to the cause, and they all made sure that Jeremiah had what he needed to get well.

"Jeremiah." Bret's dad picked Jeremiah up and held him in the air. "You're looking good, kiddo."

"I'm so glad to see those rosy cheeks and that big smile." Barbara patted him on the back and then smiled at Jason and Jill. "He looks awesome. How's his energy?"

"It's through the roof. We're so thrilled." Jill smiled at his mom, and they could all see the relief in her eyes even though she couldn't tell the whole story right there with Jeremiah in front of her. There was relief for all of them to see this child, healthy and smiling, and with pink cheeks instead of pale, drawn features. He had been through so much. Looking at him right now, it would be hard for anybody to know how much he—or Jill and Jason—had gone through.

Bret vowed then and there to continue this fight. And as his gaze moved from his friends, it collided once more with Ellie. She looked away but it was obvious she was watching him. She had been on his mind ever since their talk yesterday. He wondered what she was thinking about.

* * *

The benefit had gone great. Bret hadn't expected it to go bad; he had hoped it would be remarkable, though, and it had been. All of their friends and family who were there were amazingly generous, and the wing of the hospital would definitely be built. Although his family had been committed to making certain that would happen, it had been wonderful to watch so many people they had come to know—who were wealthy and who were not so wealthy—give what they could to make sure that the community had this new hospital wing specifically to benefit children with cancer. It had been a busy night and although he had spent time with anyone who had brought their children and wanted an autograph and also talked with anybody who was interested in giving money, he had also kept an eye on Ellie.

She had been busy, too. Her mom had run the table where there was a constant flow of women talking about—or at least, he assumed talking about—the beautiful flower decorations. He had never been one to notice things like that, but for some reason this go-around, he had noticed everything about them and had been so impressed. He had wondered just how much help Ellie had been with them. She had given all the glory to her mom on the trip the other day when they had picked the flowers up, but he had remembered his mother saying she was talented, too. And he also remembered his mother saying that Ellie's mom had wished Ellie would come home and help her grow the business.

Would Ellie consider that now since she was probably going to lose her job? Once again, guilt rode through him. But there was no way, given their history, that he wanted her to interview him. Guilt or no guilt, walking with her down memory lane just was not going to happen. There were too many things that they had been through that he didn't want to rehash in public. They were starting over, as of their recent talk, and he didn't want any misunderstandings coming up from any conversation they might have to widen the gulf between them again. He felt strongly about that.

There was dancing—not that he'd done any of it. His shoulder wouldn't have stopped him. His body wasn't hurting today. He was thankful his back, which gave him trouble sometimes, was acting right. None of that would have stopped him from dancing if he had wanted to dance; he just hadn't wanted to. He had also noticed that Ellie hadn't danced either. She had helped in the kitchen, making sure the staff was getting the hors d'oeuvres out as needed. She had made the rounds through the various businesses with tables; she had carried drinks to them when maybe the waitstaff was paying attention to the guests. And she had spent a lot of time talking with his new sisters-in-law. He had noticed that they seemed to all get along very well.

Why that mattered to him, he wasn't real sure but he did like that they seemed to be friends. Rita had been busy at her table with her new photography business/wedding planning venture. He knew this was important to her because getting weddings on board when you had started a new business was huge to anyone. Getting clientele with good sized budgets and a large client list like were here was an even bigger plus. He knew that Ellie's mom would benefit just the same. He was glad for them.

He looked at his watch. It was nearing eleven and that was when the evening would end. The band had announced one more dance and before he could talk himself out of it, he strode across the room to where Ellie talked with someone he didn't recognize.

"I hate to interrupt but, Ellie, would you like to dance?"

Her expression was shock, and he felt the flush of embarrassment as he realized she was going to turn him down.

Then the woman she was talking to smiled at him. She looked at Ellie. "Ellie, do not turn this gorgeous man down, who has given so freely, so graciously to this great cause. Go on now, you two. Enjoy this last dance." And then she had turned and walked away, with a wink toward him.

"I have to say, I don't want you to dance with me just 'cause of what she said. I didn't do all this to get a dance with you. But I just thought maybe, you know, we are starting a new chapter in our relationship…maybe this could be a dance between friends. And to celebrate that this has been a phenomenal night and the children's wing is going to get built. I haven't danced at all tonight, so I thought that it would be a great thing if you might celebrate with me."

A smile touched her lips. "Well, after all that, wouldn't I be horrible to refuse? I have to say, Bret, this has been wonderful."

He held his hand out to her; she slipped her hand into it and he pulled her out onto the dance floor. He didn't hold her close; he held her just like he would hold his sister if he had one. He danced rather stiffly, even though he was considered a really good dancer. Through the years, he had been to his share of dances, but right now this was not a time to let loose or pull her close. That would be dangerous for both of them, because he wasn't interested in anything more than the two of them at least being able to communicate and to not hold grudges against each other. Truly, that's what this was about. But as he looked into her eyes when she lifted them to his, his gut tightened and his resolve melted a little.

Surely, he wasn't interested in anything more.

CHAPTER TEN

Ellie hung up the phone. The conversation had not gone well. What had she expected? Her boss had been tremendously unhappy that she had led him along about the interview with Bret. She had really led herself along for part of that time, thinking that she could go through with it. But, in the end, she had known she would not push Bret for an interview. She'd known then that she would lose her job and as of now she had.

She sighed, standing in the backyard of her mother's home. She needed to come up with a plan.

Did she go back to Houston and look for a new job, or pack her things and move back home? Her mom wanted her here and had made that clear but was not pressuring her. Though Ellie had seen the hope in her mom's eyes that maybe, just maybe Ellie might choose to come home and go into business with her.

But was that something Ellie wanted? She just didn't know.

She walked the garden. For so long, she hadn't known what she wanted. Oh, she had wanted Bret but that had not materialized. And then she wanted her career but so much of that had been just from spite. After losing her dream of becoming Bret's wife, she had needed to become successful; she had needed a new focus somewhere far away from here, and a career had provided that for her. That old song—"How Do You Like Me Now"—played in her head. It had driven her for a while. She had clawed her way up to being semi-successful. She knew there was a lot more she could have attained if she kept at it, but did she want to?

She turned and stared at the long stretch between the back of the property and the home she had grown up in. Could she come home and live with her mom for a while? Help her mom with all the orders she had gotten from the benefit, which was amazing. She had thrown herself into helping her mom with the flower arrangements and they had been fun. She had enjoyed it. Looking at the beautiful things that she and her mom created had been satisfaction to the highest, and the flattery from everyone had actually felt good—the fact that so many people wanted them. Her mom had made sure she realized it had been their effort; people wanted them to do flowers for weddings and special occasions. It was nice. And it seemed to her even actually much more important than interviewing people who were celebrities or things like that.

She told her mom she would give her an answer in a couple of weeks. But, in the meantime, she was going to help her mother with what she had coming up. That meant she was going to be here in True Love, Texas, for a while longer. She knew that Bret had one more day before he went back to the rodeo. They had danced that last dance at the benefit. She hadn't spoken to him since but she did know that he went back on the road tomorrow. It might be a long time before she saw him again, which was good because she was getting to where she was wishing that her phone would ring and he would ask her to lunch or dinner. But her phone had not rung. She hadn't gotten a text, hadn't gotten a call; he hadn't driven by. And she didn't really want him to, did she?

Right now, she didn't need to be thinking about any of this. She pocketed her phone and strode toward the house. She needed to get to work. She had told her mom she would be in just a little bit late because she needed to make the phone call to get herself fired. She had accomplished that and now it was time to let it go and get to work. And thinking about Bret Tanner was not what she needed to be doing.

A few minutes later, she arrived in town. It was a pretty mundane day. It was ten o'clock. She could see the feed store down the road was busy, people going in and out, and she could tell that the diner on the opposite end of the road was also busy. The breakfast group was probably leaving and the early lunch group was starting to come in. She had passed the grocery store on the way in and it had also seemed fairly busy. This little town that had once been fairly dead seemed to have more people in it than it used to. Especially on a Monday morning. It was a far cry from where she lived in Houston.

She was getting out of her car when she spotted a very familiar form get out of a truck down at the feed store. *Bret.* He spotted her, too, and he waved. She waved back and tried to ignore the way that her pulse kicked up like a rampaging runaway flood.

Determined not to just stand there gawking at him, she walked to the door of the florist shop and reached to open the door.

"Ellie!"

She stopped and turned toward him, watching as he jogged halfway down the road and then walked toward her. He was grinning as he approached. The sunlight hit him straight in the face and he squinted a little against it. *Goodness, he was a gorgeous man.* He had a boyish look to his face and bright eyes, even if they were brown. There was no doubt that he still made her heart pitter-patter.

"I'm leaving tomorrow. I got a rodeo—got to ride a bull. Anyway, what do you think about maybe going to dinner tonight? I mean, you know I probably won't be back to town for a while and I hear you're going to stay. And, well, for old times' sake, what do you think?"

He was asking her on a date. Her good sense told her to say no. Her good sense screamed at her to say no. "Sure. That sounds good. For old times' sake."

He smiled. "Yeah, for both of us, this is a step forward, so I just felt like to make sure that we're stepping forward in the right direction, going out just the two of us instead of our last meeting being, you know, in a crowded place at a benefit might be a good thing."

"It sounds good. What time you going to pick me up?"

"How about six-thirty? I didn't think we'd stay in town—might drive over to Fredericksburg and get something to eat...maybe one of those outdoor restaurants. Or I can take you to a steak house if you'd like."

"No. You know I like eating outside, with some live music."

"I like live music myself. It will be a cool enough evening, so it will be nice. So six-thirty—I'll see you then. I have to go pick up some feed."

She watched him as he turned and strode away. She could barely breathe, her heart was racing so hard.

What was she doing?

Why was she looking forward to her date tonight so much?

* * *

They drove to a restaurant outside of Fredericksburg. It had decks overlooking the Guadalupe River. The cool breeze added to the great atmosphere. Their table was at the end of the deck, where they could sit and enjoy the evening, just the two of them.

Bret was a glutton for punishment, he had decided. And yet, as much as he told himself he was a fool, he had been looking forward to this evening. He had chosen a laid-back atmosphere because there was nothing stuffy about him. Every once in a while he had to put on a suit but not often. When he had on his jeans and his buckle and his boots and his button-down shirt and his hat, he was right at home. And he had to say that tonight Ellie looked as pretty as could be in a black jumpsuit, with flat sandals and sparkly bracelets and earrings. Not that he wanted to be noticing that.

"Have you enjoyed your time home?" she asked.

They had talked some about the benefit on the drive over but both of them had skirted any real issues that might be between them or anything that had to do with what might become in the future if they could forge a new friendship. But he knew that the evening couldn't continue until they opened up to each other truthfully.

"I have. I'm at a crossroads, I feel. I've had enough injuries on the rodeo circuit that I don't know how long I'll last or how beat up I want to be when I hang up my spurs. Coming home wasn't just about helping out with the benefit. It was also about me coming to terms with the reality that I see as my future. Amazingly enough, I did enjoy my time home. Whether I can get used to it on a full-time basis, I don't know. But, you know, there will come a time where it doesn't matter if I think I can or I think I can't—it will just be a reality I won't be in the rodeo anymore. 'Course, I might be on some boards or foundations with the money the family has. I can open a foundation or something that has to do with rodeo bull riding. It's not like I'm just going to stop being a part of it."

She fingered the glass of water the waitress had set before them. "Yeah, sometimes we're given ultimatums that we're not real comfortable with but we have to adjust. Like me and my journalism career. Choosing whether I want to try finding another job or do I want to stay here and go into business with my mother. I'm wanting both, but if I hadn't lost my job, I wouldn't even be considering it. So sometimes things that are out of our own understanding can make us look at things differently and consider that a change could be good."

He curled his fingers around his glass of water and lifted it to his mouth. He took a sip as his eyes held hers. *So she was thinking about staying.* She had been considering one way or the other, but he could feel it; he could feel she was thinking about staying. *And what did that do to his world?* Oddly, his heart began to thunder. "So do you have any regrets about your life? I mean, any hopes and dreams that you haven't fulfilled?" *Why was he asking her that?*

"Maybe. I want to…" She took a deep breath and he waited. "I want to move past what you and I had so that I can maybe find someone to fall in love with and have a family."

He felt a punch to the gut just then. "You mean, you haven't found someone already? Or…I don't know what I'm saying…have you been able to?" He heard the high-pitched tension in his voice that he hated. But had she been just as stuck as he had been?

"Before we messed up our relationship we were madly in love. I had given you my heart and it wasn't as easy to leave that behind as I hoped. Not that I'd ever hoped or dreamed that would be a choice I had to make but this…what we're doing now…will help. It will give me closure. And I really do want children. And I don't want to disappoint my mom but if I could find someone, I honestly think that I could maybe be just as happy being a homemaker and a mother. I think

I've been missing that fulfillment. I mean, I like my career but I got tired of going home every evening to just me and a quiet apartment. After that stretches on and on, sometimes it just gets to me. I know a lot of friends who absolutely loved it but the more I'm thinking about what I want out of my life from here on out, having a family and being a mom and a wife really makes me feel joy." She looked away, studying the water.

He leaned back in his chair. So many emotions rolled through him in that moment as pictures of the way he had envisioned their life all those years ago passed before him: him and her on a ranch, raising kids—raising rodeo kids, if they wanted—smiling, happy, and loving. His heart cinched up tight and his throat ached for things that hadn't come to pass and things that she was sitting here saying now probably wouldn't ever happen. She was looking for someone new and he needed to look for someone new. She was right—they needed to close this chapter; move on. But try as he might, he didn't see anybody in that movie that rolled through his head but her.

He smiled. "I hear ya. And maybe this will be good for you and will help you move on…get what you want."

The waitress came, of course, at that inopportune moment. But actually it was a good moment because he needed some time to grab hold of his emotions and wrangle them into submission. He ordered a steak and she ordered a salmon dish. The waitress headed out.

"Well, I'm going to leave in the morning for a rodeo. If I'm going to win NFR this year, I've got to keep getting my points to make sure I don't get beat out by some young buck, you know?"

Her eyes were serious. "I never ever thought I'd hear you say those words. You always were the young buck planning on knocking every top bull rider in the country off their pedestal, and you've just about done that. I guess time flies, though, doesn't it?"

"Yeah. Seemed like I'd have a lifetime before having to make this decision. And to be honest—seems like I keep saying that over and over again—my career hasn't been exactly what I envisioned it would be. I love it. But I don't like the blacktop—riding on it all the time and moving and traveling. I had—" He paused. He had said too much.

"What?" she asked.

"Nothing. I think I said enough. So did y'all get a lot of orders? You did, didn't you?"

They were going back to a safe conversation.

"Yes. Mom said the phones rang off the wall today. We have weddings booked and we have interviews booked with brides and other functions. A lot of benefits are looking at us now—there were a lot of social media posts. Rita is really a go-getter. And very good at social media. She's going to do well. She knows how to get noticed."

"Well, that's good. You won't be bored, right?"

"Right."

The salads came, and they ate and sipped their tea. She talked about a few funny jobs that she had had, and he talked about a few close escapes he had had. They passed the time pleasantly. He had a feeling she had as much on her mind right now as he had on his. There was a tug-of-war going on inside him. And he would manage to keep his mouth shut. He had to get a handle on this want and desire to pull her into his arms and ask her to try for what they had before. He couldn't do that, though.

When dinner was over, they headed back home. The roads were dark. It wasn't a horrible drive home but the cab inside the vehicle was quiet. The silence seemed to echo around them and he didn't know what to do about it. He was leaving tomorrow and he wasn't sure when he was coming back.

They had gone about halfway when there was trouble up ahead. They could see a car at an odd angle on the side of the road, and a man stood by the road, waving. They were not on the main highway but one of the country roads, so there wasn't a lot of traffic.

Bret immediately pulled over. "Sir, what can I help you with? Something wrong?"

"My wife. She's having a baby."

CHAPTER ELEVEN

Ellie hurried after Bret. The young cowboy was extremely stressed as they rushed to the car where, sure enough, there in the backseat was a huge, young woman with an about-to-be-born baby. Ellie had never delivered a baby. And by the way this young woman was panting and the pain written all over her face, Ellie was afraid that there was going to be a baby—and soon. She looked at Bret and, to her surprise, he looked as calm as a doctor who had done this a million times. "Bret, what are we going to do?"

He looked at the young man and put a hand on his shoulder. "All right, what's your name?"

"Dennis. And that's my wife, Gabriella."

"Okay, Dennis and Gabriella, we're going to do

this. You called 911, right?"

"I did but I don't think they're going to make it. We're way out here in the boonies."

"That's okay. As long as they are on their way, we're okay. All right, Ellie, if you'll go open my suitcase I already packed—it's in the backseat of the truck—and just grab a bunch of my shirts or something. I have a feeling we're going to need something to wrap the baby in. There's a first-aid kit in my bull-riding gear box, too…we'll need that for some supplies. And there's an ice chest in the back of my truck. Dennis, if you'll go over there and grab us a bunch of water—there's a bunch of water bottles in it. And, if you don't mind, I'll try to deliver this baby. I have delivered a lot of cows in my lifetime but, to be honest, I have never delivered a baby. But I know what to do with the umbilical cords, and I know how to catch them. I just know from the look on your face, Gabriella—you getting ready to push?"

The young woman gasped and nodded. Tears rolled down her face. "I am. I can feel it. I've never had a baby before but I feel like it's coming." She grimaced and groaned as her stomach visibly tightened. She grabbed hold of the back of the car with one hand and it was easy to see she was in a contraction.

"Hang in there, honey." He gaped at Bret. "Wait a minute—you're Bret Tanner. You're the NFR bull-riding champion."

Bret grinned. "Yeah, that I am. And I'm also about to be a midwife for your sweet wife there."

Ellie's heart was touched deeply by Bret's calm manner and easy way with the young man who was scared out of his wits.

Her thoughts rolled, Bret was the man she had loved all those years ago. She spun and hurried to the truck, not wanting to waste any more time and certainly not wanting Bret to see any indication of how he had just touched her. She opened the back door of his large, expensive truck. The seats were flipped up and his bull riding bag and suitcase lay on the floorboard. She opened the bull riding bag and pulled out the first aid kit, then she unzipped his bag and saw a full load of T-shirts. She had noticed the small suitcase when they were going to dinner. He had told her he had already packed and everything because he was leaving early in the morning.

This was going to be a long night, she feared, and he would be tired. But it was well worth it if he was about to deliver a baby. She prayed everything went well. She had confidence in him and he obviously had confidence in himself. That was one thing about Bret—he always seemed sure of everything he did. At least gave it his all. That is, he had—until it came to them.

She grabbed up some of his T-shirts that were well worn and soft. She wanted the softest she could find for the baby and whatever else he wanted. She had a feeling all of these were about to be ruined but, again, it was for a good cause. With arms full, she hurried back to the car.

Dennis jogged beside her, arms loaded with bottles of water.

"I can't believe y'all came along. I'm just so grateful. And I can't believe Bret Tanner's about to deliver my little baby. I'll never forget this. You think it will be okay?"

She smiled at him in the headlights of the truck. "Bret Tanner is going to give it his all, and you know how he is with bull riding. When he gives something his all, he usually gets the job done. I believe, like he's said, he's delivered a lot of calves—not exactly the same thing but he's got more experience than I do. And, to be honest, if I was in your wife's situation, I'd be grateful someone like Bret happened along."

Dennis looked relieved and he was nodding as if he had the shakes. "Good, good. That's what I was thinking. That's what I was hoping. I mean, I watch him ride all the time. I'm a big fan. I just—you know, it's my baby, and I got nervous there for a minute. But I know I couldn't do it. At least, I don't think I could do it. I never knew that when I got married that me and Gabriella would be facing something like this. Well, the baby is about four days early. Thank goodness it's not any earlier than that. But, anyway, that's why we're not at the hospital yet. Our sweet baby girl, she wasn't looking like she was coming two days ago when we were at the doctor's office. Doctor told us to just give it a few more days."

They had reached the car again and she saw that Bret had climbed into the backseat and was talking calmly to the young woman as he was in position. She handed him some of the shirts. "Might want to put these under her or at least right there on the seat— they'll help. And I've got some here for when the baby comes."

He looked at all of them. "Thank you very much. You two—you three—I think we're getting ready...I see a head. All right, darling, you ready? I think we're going to be ready to push, okay?"

Ellie stood there in shock as she and Dennis watched his and Gabriella's baby being born.

Bret took the little baby in his hands. His big bull-riding hands helped the sweet little baby dwarfing it. He grinned over his shoulder. "She looks good." Within moments, he had the baby and the mama separated. They wrapped the baby in the clothes, and they could hear the sirens down the road in the darkness of the still, quiet night.

It was an amazing night. Later, after he had handed over his position to the EMTs, he grinned big at Ellie. Her heart thundered and her world spun. She was in so much trouble.

"I can't believe I just delivered a baby." He held his bull-riding hand out and she saw it shake just a little bit. "I even got nervous. I don't hardly ever get nervous, but I couldn't let those two see I was nervous."

"I don't know if I've known you to be nervous. You get on the back of those humungous bulls and you're about the calmest person I've ever seen doing that. But I can see where holding a little life in your hands like that would be something to be nervous about. Thankfully you weren't as nervous as Dennis."

They both chuckled.

"No, thank goodness the good Lord helped me be steady. Goodness, what a night."

She smiled at him. "Yes, what a night. Bret, you did so good. Real good. I'm very proud of you."

He reached up and for just a moment touched her jaw with his fingertips, that he had washed and sanitized after the EMTs were there. "Thanks. And thanks for being a rock yourself. You helped Dennis stay calm and that was good."

"I didn't do anything near like what you did but I'm glad I was here to help a little bit. What a great couple."

"Yeah, that's a heck of a great beginning for them."

"Yes. Starting a family with excitement like that…everything else from here on out is going to be gravy to them."

He smiled. "Yeah, I hope so. If that had been me in his position, I don't think I'd be as calm as I was delivering someone else's baby. If it was me trapped on the side of the road with my wife about to give birth in a car, I probably would have been freaking out too."

Her heart suddenly ached. If things had been the way they had been years ago, he would've been talking about her being in the back of that car, having their baby. But that wasn't ever going to happen.

* * *

Bret had delivered a baby. He might be acting as if he

hadn't been nervous but he had been nervous—more nervous than any other time in his life. Delivering a precious new baby was not the same as delivering a calf, no matter how much he had acted that just because he had delivered a calf he could deliver a baby. No, he had just wanted to try to put some calm in the situation, which, thankfully, he had been able to do. And it calmed him too.

Now, he stood beside Ellie and watched the young mother and baby--Gabriella and baby Grace loaded into the ambulance. Dennis had tears in his eyes as he turned and, without any shame threw his arms around Bret and hugged him tight thanking him profusely for saving his wife and baby and for coming along and for being such a great guy. Then the new daddy ran to his car and followed the ambulance as it was heading down the road.

Bret's own emotions nearly failed him at that moment because he had never had such a heartfelt thank-you for anything, not that he had ever done anything more important than what he had done tonight. He was in awe; he was humbled. And he felt as though he might never do anything as important in his life again.

"You were wonderful, Bret."

Ellie's quiet voice in the darkness as the ambulance lights disappeared around the corner had him taking a deep breath, and he turned to her. "I just did what needed to be done. Thank you for helping to be calm in such a non-calm situation."

She gave him a tender smile that touched his heart. "You didn't need me, Bret. You were amazing, just like Dennis said in that sweet, emotional thank-you that he gave you. I started crying myself."

"I almost cried myself. It was amazing. Not me—just the whole situation was amazing. And just think—God put us here on this road at this particular time so we could help bring that baby into the world. I don't think that was an accident. He put us here, and I'm humbled by that fact."

"I believe it. And I am, too, but I just gave you some T-shirts out of your own suitcase. You did everything. It was amazing, and I guess we can stand here all night saying that. I just…"

"What?" He heard wishfulness in her voice.

As she studied the darkness where the ambulance

had disappeared, she said, "It just makes me more certain that I want a family. I've been missing out so much. I want a family so bad."

"I do too."

They stared at each other, neither of them saying anything more. He wondered what she was thinking. He wondered whether she was having regrets like he did. Now wasn't the time to talk about that; they just made long strides toward a new beginning—a friendship—and he didn't need to let this miraculous event that had happened tonight falter their tender progress.

"So I guess we both know, we each want to move forward so we can have a family. I'm glad we've decided to move forward from our past. Now maybe we'll move forward with everything else."

"Yeah, that would be nice."

"And, on that note, I've got an early start in the morning. I'm driving this rig to Denver instead of flying, and I need to be there by tomorrow evening, so I've got to be up early."

"Of course. Then we better head back."

He had already said all that because they wanted to go to the hospital and see the baby, but they also didn't want to intrude too much. So they had told Dennis when he had asked them to come to the hospital that they would keep in touch and when he got back from the rodeo, maybe he could come by and see the baby. Dennis had wholeheartedly agreed to that.

They walked back to the truck. He held the door for Ellie as she climbed in and then closed it, not letting himself linger—not letting himself reach up and touch the soft cheek that he wanted to touch. Or kiss those pretty lips he wanted to kiss. Because there was no denying that he wanted to—terribly bad. *Nope*. He strode around the front of the truck, climbed in the driver's seat and, without another word, headed home.

CHAPTER TWELVE

Ellie walked into the restaurant in Fredericksburg and spotted Tulip Tanner and Rita Tanner at a table across the room, waiting for her. They both smiled as she threaded her way through the restaurant to take the seat. They already had a glass of water sitting next to the napkins. It had been nearly a week since she and Bret had gone on their date and delivered a baby. Well, Bret had delivered a baby—she watched in awe.

It had been a crazy, odd week. She and her mother had been working hard and she had been startled to see how her mother pushed the newly developing business that had to do with the wedding planning and photography business into her lap. Her mother had insisted that she trusted her and wanted this to be her baby, that she was content to stay at the shop and work behind the scenes. That was where she wanted to be. As strange as it sounded, after her mother had really been pushing to enlarge the business, Ellie could see that her mother meant it.

Ellie wondered whether this was her mother's plan all along, that she was expanding the business for Ellie, taking the business into a more exciting venue of weddings and parties and not just doing funerals. It was hard to see friends and family dying in a small town and being surrounded by funeral flowers—it had depressed Ellie. Doing flowers for weddings and parties added a happier dimension to the rather one-sided business that had been her mother's.

This new venture gave Ellie a rather intriguing and fun aspect, because she would be meeting a lot with Rita and also Tulip, who, with her landscaping skills, was also creative and she was coming into the business. They were all joining forces to have a partnership of sorts. Ellie was finding it exciting. Plus, she really liked both women and was thrilled that they seemed to be forging a friendship rather than just a business partnership. The fact that they were married to Tanner brothers and that she had a past history with a Tanner brother added an element of complication, in her mind, to the situation. And part of that complication was that she didn't have any kind of idea of what she and Bret were doing at the moment.

He had left that next day, headed for Denver, and then had had his rodeo the following night. Her phone had rung after a quick text at about eleven-thirty, wondering whether she was still up. She had texted him that she was and he had called. Strangely enough, they had talked for about an hour about his winning that night, about still not being over having delivered a baby and the miracle of it all. Then she had hung up and she had gone to sleep, something that had eluded her until the call that night. She had been wondering how he had done at the rodeo. He had been on her mind and she had been glad that he had called, because the event hadn't been televised, and she had been glad for him that he had won. And that he was healthy and hadn't hurt his shoulder again.

Then, the next night, he had called while he was driving to his next destination, which was one reason he had taken his truck up. He had several rodeos within driving distance. He preferred that over flying. And he liked having his own pickup, if he could. He was a creature of habit and familiarity, she remembered that much.

And then, last night he had called again. They were just being friendly—that was it…just talking. But she was shocked at, after agreeing to move past their history, how easily they had been able to fall back into talking to each other. And today she was having lunch with his sisters-in-law. She couldn't help feeling a bit strange that once she had believed she would be one of the Tanner women.

"We are so glad you made it!" Rita said as she sat down.

"This is going to be a great adventure for all of us." Tulip smiled as she took a sip of her water, her eyes dancing. "Once we put it out there that we're throwing our talents together, I've had several calls from people who want me to do their floral gardens in preparation for weddings. So we can work to get the photography, flowers, and even the wedding planning itself for those events."

"I'm excited about it, and that's wonderful that you're getting calls like that. I can't wait. I'm so glad that I have decided to help Mom out, at least for now."

Both of them looked slightly alarmed. They shot glances to each other, and then Rita spoke first. "So you're not sure if you're going to continue? I just think it would be wonderful."

"I didn't mean to scare you like that, but I just originally agreed to help Mom. Then she wanted me to play point on it with y'all and I'm thrilled. I think it's going to be amazing. But no, I haven't completely made up my mind about if I'm going to go back to journalism or, you know, something that has to do with my writing. Although I am excited about this, so who knows? We'll see."

"Well, we can't ask any more than that." Tulip smiled at her. Such a pleasant person—she always seemed positive.

Positive—Ellie needed to think more positive

herself. She liked the idea and she liked them, so why did she have to say that a moment ago? Why was she still hesitant about whether she was going to commit to this?

Of course, she knew it was that complication—that relationship she had with Bret and the uncertainty of whether they could truly forge this friendship, especially if it was just to be a friendship. If he moved forward and found someone new, would she be able to stay on in True Love, Texas, watching him and his true love and it not be her? That, she knew, was going to be the deciding factor.

"All right, so, anyway, let's just not think about that. This is all about us getting this business going. With all these orders and requests about it, I'm excited about moving forward."

"All right then, then we're excited too." Rita laughed. She opened her menu when the waitress walked up. "I'm going to have your strawberry-pecan spinach salad, with raspberry vinaigrette dressing, please, and chicken."

They all ordered, feeling upbeat and happy. After

the waitress left, they discussed some of the upcoming events. One of them was the following weekend. And then they had a major wedding booked further out, but several small charity events that they could handle. They coordinated their calendars. By the time the meal had come, they had each closed their calendars and agreed that Rita would coordinate them on their shared calendar, and then they settled in for the meal.

After Rita had taken a few bites, she set her fork down and took a drink of her lemon water. "So, Levi told me that Bret had mentioned that he had called you. I mean, it makes sense after y'all delivered that sweet baby together that you would be talking. We don't particularly know everything because everyone's real close-lipped about it, but we do know that you and Bret once dated, like, seriously."

Tulip had set her fork down, too, and took a sip of water, and then dabbed her napkin against her mouth. "We don't want to intrude but we can't help but be curious. I mean, it just seems like at the benefit the other night that you and Bret did seem to maybe have something still between you two."

This was that complication again. She hesitated, considering how in the world to answer them. They were the closest thing to friends she had right now. Sure, she had gone to school in True Love—it was a very small school—but most of her classmates had moved on. Not that many people settled in True Love after they graduated. Therefore, she didn't have many people who actually knew exactly how long she had been with Bret.

"Yes, we were friends and attracted in high school but didn't start dating until the end of the year after high school. With work on the ranch and rodeoing on the side he was very busy. "

"My Toby's enrolled this year in his first year of school—you know, kindergarten—and it is a very tiny class. Although, it is a bigger class than the graduating class. That seems to diminish as the kids get older. I guess they move on and things like that."

"Yes, I went to school all twelve of my years there, and so did all of the Tanner boys." She hadn't answered the question yet, but maybe they would just move on now that they had talked that through. She wasn't so lucky as Rita smiled.

"So y'all dated seriously and then y'all broke up? From what Levi said, he had thought maybe y'all would get married."

"Right. We had thought so, too. But, you know, things don't always work out like you believe they will. We were young and Bret had the NFR on his mind, and when he sets a goal, he reaches for it."

Rita and Tulip exchanged glances again.

Trying not to feel awkward, Ellie took a bite of her salad. It really was delicious. And fresh. The vinaigrette was amazing and the candied pecans mixed with the spinach and the grilled chicken—it was a lovely meal. But it didn't take away the uncomfortable feeling that she felt as her two new friends looked from each other back to her.

Tulip reached across and patted her hand. "Love is complicated, isn't it? Y'all were too young because he had hopes and dreams, and your love didn't quite make it through. What about now?"

"There is no now. We've just made it past the awkwardness of our situation. I guess we've both matured."

Rita smiled and her eyes twinkled. "Believe me, I know about immaturity. I married my first husband out of immaturity and stupidity. He was a jerk and although I was blessed to get my Toby out of the fiasco of a marriage, I have to say that sometimes youth can get in the way of clarity and decision-making. Maybe you two have regrets that y'all broke up?"

Regrets? Oh yes, most definitely there were regrets. "Maybe. But really, y'all, I'm not even sure what to say. Right now, we're really just navigating the new waters of friendship. So I don't have anything else to tell you two." She hoped with all her heart they understood, and her refusing to talk about it didn't hurt their new friendship.

"Fair enough," Tulip said. "But you just know we're here for you. And if you ever need to talk, you can talk to us. We can hold confidentiality, you know."

"Absolutely," Rita said. "Just because we're married to two of the Tanner boys doesn't mean they have to know everything we talk about, so if you and Bret end up moving past this new waters of friendship that y'all are wading in and you wade into deeper waters and you need somebody to throw some conversation at…you know, to help you understand those muddied waters…we're your girls. We've got your back, not just in business but in this too. We like you and we think… Well, maybe I'm talking too much." Rita's nose scrunched up as she bit her lip.

Ellie laughed. "Don't feel uncomfortable. Thank you both. I really appreciate you being there and understanding. And I'll let you know if we wade into any deeper waters and I need you. That's comforting to know."

And it was. Except they just didn't know how muddy the water was.

CHAPTER THIRTEEN

Bret drove from Billings toward Springfield, Missouri. It was a nice seventeen-hour drive, and as he drove, he wondered why he thought this was a bright idea. Of course, the drive from Texas to Billings had been the long haul; this was a short one compared to that one. But he had needed the drive. Something about riding a horse or making a drive—despite how much he hated the road—gave him time to think. And he must have known he needed time to think when he decided to bring his truck on this trip. And, of course, what was he thinking about but Ellie?

She had been on his mind ever since he had gotten in that truck a week ago and headed toward Billings. And she was still on his mind. He had been unable to stop himself from picking up the phone that night after he won the rodeo event. He had called her before he could back out. When he had texted her, he almost wished she had been asleep and missed his text, but nope, she had texted him right back that she had wanted to know how he'd done. And of course he talked to her—he had picked that phone up and dialed her number so fast. It had felt good to share with her how he had done. It felt like the old days, when he had first gone on the road, with his heart full and his hopes high. He had called her, and they had talked and talked. She had encouraged him and they had shared in this dream of his. It had felt like the right thing back then.

But he knew, little by little, just like the weariness of the road had weighed on him, loneliness had driven him to have more conversations with female rodeo athletes than he would have had if Ellie had been with him. But back then, there was no way Ellie could have been with him, unless they were married. Neither one of them were the type to live together and back then it just wasn't what needed to be done. He hadn't meant anything by talking to the girls, but the tabloids had grabbed hold of those pictures and blown them all out of proportion. Yup, the failure of their relationship weighed on his shoulders and he knew it.

But even knowing that, he knew that this felt right. He had to play his cards right. He had to fix this. He had done enough thinking to know what he wanted, and what he wanted was Ellie. Plain and simple. If she would want him.

He looked at the clock on the dashboard. It was eight o'clock; it had just turned dark and he knew he was going to drive a couple more hours before he called it a night. And he knew what was niggling at him. But again, either he couldn't stop himself or—truth was—he didn't want to stop himself. He tapped the call button steering wheel to call Ellie on his phone. It connected instantly.

"Hello, Bret."

His heart thundered, and his hands kind of got damp holding the steering wheel. "Ellie, I'm driving and I just thought I'd call and see how you are."

"I'm good." The smile in her voice was evident.

He smiled. "I'm glad. I had an idea. I'm not sure if I should or if I shouldn't, but I was wondering if I sent a plane for you tomorrow, what would you think about coming to the rodeo?"

"You couldn't do that. It's all the way in Springfield."

"I can send a plane for you and, on a plane, it's a real short flight. I'd be at the rodeo ring, so I'd have a car pick you up, bring you right there to the rodeo, and depending on what time you got there, I might be able to see you before the ride. You know, bull riding's always late. Then maybe we could have a late dinner afterward and I could either get you a hotel room or, if you needed to get back, I can have the plane wait for you. You could sleep on the plane and then I'll have a car deliver you right to your house."

"I don't know, Bret. I'm not used to that."

"Look, I'm not trying to sway you but really, I've got all this stinking money and I don't know what to do with it. If I can get a friend of mine a seat on a charter plane to fly out and watch me in a rodeo and have dinner with me just because, well, 'cause I can't take you out on a date myself, I think that's a good way to spend some of that money."

She laughed and he heard in that laugh a little less hesitation.

"Come on, Ellie. You know, it's been feeling good, talking the last few nights. At least, it has for me. And you've been bringing me luck. I've had some of the best rides I've had since I injured myself, and I'm going to say that's all because of you. My spirits are feeling good and my shoulder feels great. It feels a little bit like old times."

"It's not old times, though, and maybe we don't need to get mixed up about that, Bret."

"Okay, forget I said that. I didn't mean to mess things up. I just meant, well, you know, back in the day, we enjoyed talking about the rodeo together and just…I don't know. Something about talking to you puts me at ease and kind of relaxes me, you know?"

"I remember how you used to always say that. But really, you've done well without conversations with me and there's no denying that."

He felt his gut twist a little on that one. She didn't

know that he had done well not because it came easily, but that it was by brute force, and he had always missed what they had had. "Come on, Ellie. You'd enjoy it. My family flies out every once in a while to see me ride, but it's not like they can stop their lives and follow me around the rodeo circuit. It's a heck of a lot of road time. I know some families do it but, you know, I'm a man. I don't need my family following me around, but every once in a while it's nice to have someone in the stands other than friends and family of other people." He didn't want to sound like he was begging, but he really wanted Ellie to come to Springfield. And it was nothing to pick up a phone and call his friend who owned the charter service.

He didn't say anything and the miles ticked by. He heard a shuffling noise and waited despite wanting to push further.

"Okay, I can do that. What time should I be ready?"

A huge smile erupted across his face and he had to hold back a yelp of joy. "I don't think the flight's very long. I can text you the details, but I'm excited. What time do you think? If I had the plane there by three or four, that gets you here by…oh shoot, that probably gets you here by…I don't know what the flight time is but maybe by six. I can see you for just a few minutes before I have to get back and start doing my stretching."

"Okay, then I'll be waiting at three. You're going to have a car pick me up or do I need to drive to the airport?"

"No, I'll get my buddy, Beck McCoy, who has the charter service—he'll fly you. I'll send a car to pick you up and take you to their private landing strip, so no need to plan anything on your end."

"I can't believe I'm doing this."

"I can't either but I'm glad. So I'll get you a room—or you want the plane to wait and take you home that night?"

He wanted her to get a room. It would be a late night but he wasn't going to push.

"I'll get a room because it will be late, especially if we leave there and have dinner somewhere. I don't know where in the world you're going to find dinner at that hour besides an all-night fast-food restaurant."

"You let me worry about that. I'll have your room ready. I'll let you know where and I'll take you back there as soon as we have dinner."

"Okay, then. I guess we have a plan."

Oh yeah, they had a plan.

* * *

A gleaming limousine picked Ellie up the next afternoon. She learned from the older man who was driving that he was Mr. Talbert McCoy's personal driver and that he and his limousine were at the McCoy ranch just down the road most of the time. "I drive some but on other days, when he goes into Dallas or Houston or wherever he goes for his business, I drop him off at the airport like I'm about to do you—the private airport at the McCoy ranch—and then I pick him up. Someone else drives him in the big city. I'm semi-retired and enjoying it. But I have to say, I'm enjoying coming and picking you up today, ma'am. You look lovely. I hear you're going to a rodeo."

She smiled as she sat down in the backseat and looked up at him. He was all spiffy in his immaculate limousine driving uniform and he looked like he thoroughly enjoyed what he did. "Thank you for picking me up, and I am going to a rodeo. First rodeo I've been to in years."

"Well, everybody needs to go to a rodeo every once in a while. And I hear that you're going to watch that talented Bret Tanner ride, so that should be an interesting rodeo to see tonight. I'm going to get you there safe and sound, okay?" He tapped his hat, closed the door, and then climbed into the front seat. "Make sure you buckle up."

She did just that, and then he pressed the gas and they were off.

When they got to the airport, it was a private place at the back of the McCoy Winery. The small jet looked as though it sat on the runway, waiting for her. She got out and Beck McCoy, who she had met at the benefit the other night, came down the steps and greeted her. Within moments, they were in the air.

This lifestyle. Flying places like this was not

something she was used to but it certainly beat going to the airport in Austin or San Antonio and getting on a flight and having to do a connection probably and then flying on to Springfield. So she sat back and sipped on her glass of tea that Beck had offered her before they got in the air and enjoyed the ride. When she reached Springfield, again it was a private airport and a limo waited there for her. Within moments, she was at the event center. Her luggage was being swept away to the hotel and then the limo driver had informed her that he would pick her up the next morning for a flight back. She had thanked him and now stood in the crowded venue, watching the competitors move back and forth, getting ready for their events.

She nearly jumped when someone tapped her on the shoulder and she spun to find Bret grinning at her.

"Hey, it's good to see you." He leaned forward and gave her a quick hug.

It was just a hug between friends—that's all it was, she told herself as she felt the urge to hold on tight and make it more than that. But she had more pride than that and released him.

He released her and stepped back. "Glad you made it in time. I pulled a good one. It should be a great ride. I pulled the bull everybody wants. He'll make me put on a good show. And make me some big points—exactly what I need."

She tried to not let her crazy emotions that had started suddenly overwhelm her. She was here, actually about to watch him compete. This had been their dream. He would make it big and she would be there for him. But that had never happened. Not once after he went to start competing in the pro bull-riding events had she ever been there. Just others who he said were just people he talked to…and the tabloids had said it was more.

"I'm excited to be here." She hoped her voice didn't wobble and that she sounded like she was glad to be here. She was going to have a good time—she was. She was not going to let her emotions get the better of her.

* * *

"Again, I'm really glad you're here. I'm going to have

to get back down there and do my stretches and get prepared, but I'm going to have Eddie over there—see the older man over there, standing to the side, being very discreet? That's Eddie. He's going to take you up to your seat. We're going to eat late. I'm not sure if you've eaten anything, but there's food there in the box and you can have whatever you want. It's going to be a few hours. I didn't know if you wanted to be in a box with people or without, so there are a few other bull riders' families up there, too. I hope that's okay?"

"Oh, it's fine."

"Most of them are wives, so I tend to always get a private booth when I have family coming. I always invite the wives of some of the other guys to sit there, too. So, anyway, I hope that works."

"It does. Good luck, and I'll be rooting for you." Excitement filled her and he grinned. She was excited for him. He had wanted this for so long and she knew from what he'd said the other day that after the injury that damaged his shoulder, it plagued him and he needed his shoulder to stay on the back of the bull.

The evening went well. There were several young

wives and a few children in the booth, all excited to watch their dads and their husbands compete. She thought it was nice that there was a camaraderie there between them; they were friends even though their husbands competed against one another. She assumed that they each wanted to win the prize, so she didn't quite understand the dynamic. But she was glad to see the people in the room were excited for each other, and when one of the guys got hurt, they were there for the young woman as she stood there, terrified for her husband who had just gotten thrown from a bull. He landed in a very awkward position and was surrounded by rodeo clowns protecting him as the cowboys on horses herded the bull out of the arena. Tense moments passed and then the young man was helped to his feet, to the relief of everyone. He turned toward the booth, waving his hat and grinning up at his wife, Carrie. She nearly fainted with relief.

Immediately, all the other women hugged Carrie and shared in her relief and her happiness. That was the first moment that Ellie was reminded of the danger of what Bret did. Her stomach churned as his time approached. Sicily and Esmerelda, two of the wives who were sitting beside her, explained that he had drawn the top bull to ride, but also the meanest bull on the circuit. They believed Bret had ridden it before and come out on top, but it was no easy job.

But when someone did ride that particular bull, the points were usually high and that was the reason so many of them wanted to give it a go. Others who might not be quite as talented as Bret, who were clinging to their points to make it to the top and being in the money, weren't always as keen to get the top bull like that because being damaged by the bull could cost them everything.

Bret was different. There had been no fear in Bret's voice when he had told her the bull he'd drawn. No, there had been no fear, no anxiety—just excitement and the thought of the thrill of the ride. She had to remind herself that Bret Tanner was one of the best. Still, as she sat there and waited through the next three bull rides, her anxiety level rose. Her hands were clasped in her lap as she waited. When he finally came into view, she could see him on the big screen and down in the shoot. She watched him from the big screen because from the box they were sitting in, he was quite a ways down there. And from the big screen, she could see his face. Again, there was no fear—just serious contemplation as he looked down in the shoot at the bull. He tugged on his glove, straightened his hat, and then climbed over the railing. The bull jumped and he climbed back out. The bull was restless. She had seen many a cowboy do this earlier: they waited for the bull to settle before they settled on the bull's back.

This bull was not settling. He was not happy about being in that small chute.

She watched again as Bret tugged on his glove, making it tighter. Again, he straightened his hat, almost as if this was just his ritual, and then he climbed back over the ledge. This time, he put one leg on the far railing so that he was in a position to straddle the bull. Then, as one of the men held onto his protective vest on the back—which she knew meant he could help pull Bret out if he needed to—Bret eased himself onto the back of the bull. The bull jumped but Bret didn't move. He slipped his gloved hand palm up beneath the strap, then he wound the rope around his hand. Bret kept his head down—she knew he was settling in—and then he nodded and lifted his hand into the air.

That gave the signal; the chute opened and the bull lunged sideways, then up into the air. It kicked its hind legs up into the air and it spun and spun. Bret held on like a dancer in a violent, orchestrated dance. Bret moved with the animal, his arm up in the air. He leaned back; he leaned forward. The bull spun and spun and kicked back and forth, throwing Bret forward and then back. And yet Bret moved his legs, riding with the animal, giving a show.

She knew as she watched that he was a master at what he did. No wonder he showed no fear. She could see in the eight-second ride, the determination on his features, the concentration and the love for what he did. When the buzzer rang, he slipped his hand from beneath the rope, threw his leg over and jumped to the ground, moving out of the way of the rampaging bull as riders rode to divert the bull away from him. He turned toward the booth, grabbed his hat, and lifted it in salute—to her, she knew.

And then he bowed and the arena went wild.

She smiled with relief. Esmerelda and Sicily were clapping, and they were all standing and she accepted their hugs even though she was still in dismay and frozen to the spot. "He did it."

"Oh yes, he did do it," Esmerelda exclaimed. "That was a heck of a ride. It's going to be a high score."

"That's what he said he wanted from it."

"Well, let's just see what it turns out to be. But I'm sure he got what he wanted."

And sure enough, the score was the winning score of the night. By the time the show was over, her heart was still pounding as she was escorted down to the area where Bret was. She entered a room and saw Bret sitting on a massage table. His shirt was off and there was a masseuse trainer applying an ice pack to his shoulder and winding it around his shoulder with plastic wrap, latching it into place. Bret grinned at her even though she paused in the doorway, not having expected to see him being attended to.

"Hey, we did it! It was a great ride."

"It was. Are you okay?"

"Oh, yeah. This is just a precaution. My shoulder's always bothering me. It hurts like a son of a gun, so we have to ice it down. You know, if you don't ice it down, it will swell up and I'll be incapacitated for days. But getting it iced up like this will ease it off and get me on the road down to the next one."

She knew this was normal for him. And yet it reminded her that he couldn't possibly do this forever. Like a football player or a hockey player or any of the athletes who were in aggressive sports—their bodies just didn't last.

"You give me a few minutes and we're going to head out. I decided to get the limo to come back and pick us up. I had them take my truck to my hotel. I'm staying the same place you are, but I've got us separate rooms. So we can eat and then head up so you can get back tomorrow. Don't you have an event?"

"I do, but the majority of it's done, so Mom and everybody were all on board for me to come tonight, so it's fine. I'll get back by noon or one and then I'll have plenty of time."

He grinned. "Great. I'm excited that you came. Really excited."

She smiled, feeling both melancholy at how things had not turned out as they planned all those years ago and an excitement about what could be happening between them now.

CHAPTER FOURTEEN

Bret had chosen the nicest hotel in town and he had requested a late-night dinner on a private patio overlooking the city.

He wasn't trying to impress Ellie or romance Ellie. Actually, he just wanted her stay to be nice and he wanted them to have an enjoyable late-night evening. He was starving and she hadn't eaten very much during the rodeo, so she had to be too. So with nothing but fast-food restaurants open this late, this was their only option. Normally he might just grab a snack in his cheaper motel. He wasn't into staying in the most ritzy places, despite that the Tanner money would have enabled him to do that. He was a rodeo guy and he liked to be that.

"We're going up the elevator and then to a private patio that they use for special events. I booked it so we could have a nice dinner instead of a meal in the bar with a lot of late-night drunks. I figured that would be better than bar food, anyway, and after you flew all this way, I didn't want you to go back with a hamburger, you know? I hope it's okay?"

She walked onto the elevator when the door opened, and turned and smiled at him. "I think it sounds great. I really wasn't looking forward to a hamburger after this long day. But, honestly, the bar food would have been fine. I could have gotten anything other than a hamburger. But this is very nice and thoughtful, so thank you. You've really gone out of your way for me on this trip."

The door closed with a ding and he pushed the button to the twentieth floor.

"Well, like I said, after you agreed to fly out this far, I didn't want to mistreat you. Only thing I had to do was preorder a meal, so hopefully what I ordered will be okay with you."

"I'm sure it will be great. So are you sore right now?"

He rotated his shoulder—normally he would have still had an ice pack on, but he had opted to take it off for tonight. He'd pay for it tomorrow probably, but that would be okay. "Yeah, I'm good. I'll be sore but that's just part of the game."

The elevator door dinged open and they stepped out to a lighted room with lots of tables with chairs on top of them as the room was not being used. Across the room, near the lighted window, stood a waiter. They walked toward him. He greeted them and pushed open the door. They walked out onto the balcony. There, a single table had been set exquisitely. A covered platter sat at each seating area. He had texted when they had entered the building that they were on their way up, so the meal had been ready. He hadn't wanted them to have to wait while the whole meal was readied because he was afraid she had been starving, and though he could have probably talked all night, he hadn't wanted to infringe on her time. She had a full day tomorrow to get back to True Love and the wedding that she and his sisters-in-law and her mother were involved with.

After the waiter had poured their drinks, took the

platter lid off, and asked them whether they needed anything else, he discreetly moved back into the building and turned his back on them. He would be there if they needed anything but with the smile on Ellie's face as she saw the dish, he didn't figure they would need anything else.

"I cannot believe you remembered."

"I always remembered you liked beef stroganoff with garlic bread and buttery grilled asparagus with parmesan. I hope this is okay?"

She laughed.

He loved the sound of it.

"Would you quit asking me if it's okay? It's fantastic. I'll probably eat every bit of this and pay for it in the morning by weighing ten pounds extra because we're eating so late. But I'm going to enjoy every bite. I'm certain that the chef at this restaurant knows exactly what he's doing to prepare this."

"Actually, one reason I chose this particular hotel was they were able to accommodate my late-night dinner wants. And two, I've heard great things about his stroganoff. It's not usually the most popular dish in high-class restaurants, but this guy supposedly knows what he is doing."

"Then I hope you don't mind, I'm going to dig in."

"Yeah, that's great. If you don't mind, I'd like to say a quick blessing."

Her expression softened. "Sure, I would like that."

He bowed his head, thanked the good Lord for a safe bull ride but most especially for Ellie's presence, that she would have a good evening and that she would have safe travels home tomorrow, and then he thanked the Lord for her friendship and that their path to renewing their friendship would be a blessing. He hoped he hadn't said too much, but when he finished, he just looked across at her. "All right, I meant all of that, you know. I'm glad we're starting to be friends again. Now let's dig in."

She looked as though she were going to say something but didn't. Instead, she picked up her fork and twirled it in the stroganoff, lifted it to her mouth and took a bite. He did the same.

The evening went well. They talked again about

their past—her job and he told stories of his rides—and they avoided personal issues. He wasn't sure whether they would always avoid them, but right now, in the beginning at least, they needed to get this footing underneath them. Get comfortable with each other again—just be friends. And later, as he escorted her to her room, he wasn't sure what to do. But, in the end, as she unlocked her door and then turned to him, he hugged her, briefly. Oh, he wanted to hug her longer but he just gave her a brief, friendly hug, let her go, and backed away with a scent of peaches and cream in his nostrils.

He tipped his hat. "I'll see you in the morning. You said you'll be getting up and heading toward the airport at nine. We'll have breakfast, so I'll meet you at seven-thirty here. Or in the dining room? No, I'll come here and get your bag for you, okay?"

"Okay. I'll see you in the morning." She stepped inside and started to close the door.

He turned and started down the hall. His room was purposefully across the hall but down a ways. He hadn't wanted to crowd her.

"Bret," she called, and he turned back to her.

"This was a great evening. Really good. Good night." And then she closed the door.

He just stood there, looking at that closed door. His heart hammered; his gut twisted and a small, faint flicker of hope kindled in his heart.

* * *

Over the next three weeks, Ellie thought of that evening with Bret almost continuously. She thought of how carefully he had orchestrated it to be perfect for her and his hug at the end of the evening. He had escorted her to the limo that morning and then given her another very brief hug and told her to be safe. She hadn't seen him since then. He had been on the road, racking up points at any rodeo he could get to. And he was making his sponsors happy; he had ads to do and yet he had called her briefly almost every other night. She could have enjoyed him calling every night, but she didn't say so. She didn't want to seem eager or too hopeful that what they were doing could possibly lead to anything more serious.

Their picture had made it into the tabloids the night after their meeting in Springfield. There had been speculation as to whether billionaire Bret Tanner had a new woman in his life. It was not like she realized he hadn't been photographed with any women on his arm in a while. Had he slowed down his dating? Because she knew over the years, since they had split up, he had been linked to several women; it just had never stuck. Thankfully, the interest hadn't been enough to bring the paparazzi to town as far as she could tell, and Tulip and Rita told her that was surprising. But then again, there was a whole big thing going on in Hollywood with the release of a giant movie and one of the big couples there were splitting up, so thankfully most of the paparazzi attention was there—giving her and Bret a reprieve.

She and her mom, along with Rita and Tulip, had been busy over these last three weeks. First, she'd gone to Houston and had her apartment loaded up and brought back to her mom's and stored in the barn until she found a place of her own. She hadn't spent much time on the move as she and the ladies had a lot to get done. They had several weddings and several rehearsal parties, and other events that they had prepared flowers for and taken photos of and just helped plan in general. So it wasn't that she could have actually even flown to another rodeo, if he had even asked her, but she was hoping for another invitation. She was ready to see him again and not just to have a conversation.

Her mother had already left the shop for the day, but she had stayed behind to finish up some estimates for a wedding they would be doing the flowers for in a few weeks, if they got the bid. Thankfully, though, she had upped her mother's prices a little because her mother had been overworking herself and not charging enough for her services compared to the going rate. She was ready to call it a day. She had just locked the door and turned toward her car when a truck with *Tanner Ranch* painted on the door pulled into the parking space beside her. Her heart leapt in her chest when she recognized the driver.

"Hey there, pretty lady." Bret leaned out the window and grinned at her.

Trying not to appear overly excited, she smiled.

"Well, hey there, cowboy. What brings you to town? I thought you would be in Timbuktu or somewhere, riding a bull."

"No can do. I ride tomorrow night. And, to be honest, I needed a trip home, so I called my buddy and he flew his plane in and dropped me off an hour ago, and here I am. I was wondering if you would like to go to dinner?"

He had flown into town to take her to dinner? Was she putting too much into his statement? Maybe he missed his parents. No, they weren't in town. His brothers? Could he have missed her like she missed him? Hope unfurled inside her. "I don't know. My schedule's pretty full." His look of disappointment made her heart thump a little faster. "I'm just teasing. I would love to go to dinner. I'm actually starved. I skipped lunch today."

"Well, if that's the case, I'll take you whenever you're ready. Wouldn't want to keep the lady waiting."

"Let me just put my briefcase in the car."

"If you're that hungry, you have anything against just going over to Manny's?"

"Manny's is great. I love their menu."

Within minutes, she was in the truck and they had driven the six miles out to the bar and grill.

Manny had happened to be working behind the bar area when they walked in. The old man grinned from ear to ear. "Well, look who it is. Seems like old times, seeing you two walk in together."

She wasn't exactly sure how to answer that but she just smiled at the old man. "Hey, Manny. How are you doing?"

He was wiping out glasses. "Oh, I'm doing great. Just getting ready for the evening crowd. But, you know, on a Thursday night, it's not as busy as Friday and Saturday night, so y'all go back there and pick whatever table or booth you want."

He winked and she blushed. Memories of them as two lovebirds hurrying back to find a booth heated her cheeks.

"Thanks, Manny. We'll be at the back. Just a couple waters to start with and no rush."

They headed to the back and took a corner booth.

"So is this going to make you too tired for tomorrow night?"

He shrugged. "Nah, I'm okay. I decided that a trip home would do me better than sleep, so here I am. Jake needed a little help in the morning on a project he's working on at the ranch, so I decided that was the last part of the excuse I needed to come on back and see if you would go to dinner with me." His expression was almost boyish.

"Well, to be honest, I'm glad. I've missed talking to you, Bret. I mean, not talking to you but seeing you."

His expression turned serious. "I've missed you too. I think I'm kind of relieved to hear you say that. I… I have been enjoying our phone conversations. I've enjoyed hearing how well you've been doing the last three weeks with y'all's new business adventure. But even the couple of times we FaceTimed, it's still not like having a face-to-face chat, you know?"

"I know exactly what you're saying."

Their waters came and the waitress asked them what they wanted. He wanted a medium-rare steak and she ordered a well-done steak. They laughed; they were such opposites when it came to how they liked their steaks grilled. But sometimes opposite likes and dislikes were a good thing.

He told her about an encounter he had had during the filming of a commercial where the little boy in the commercial was supposed to be looking up to him. He was a cute little kid, and they had had to redo the commercial several times because the little boy was truly a fan and nervous.

"He was so cute." Bret laughed. "I had to finally just stop the commercial and take the little kid out to sit at a table and have a soda with me, and we just talked for a little while. Poor little kid had to get used to me and realize I was a regular person. We would have never gotten through that commercial if he hadn't gotten comfortable with me. I think by the time I did that, it had been the fifteenth or sixteenth take, and I'm not one to do thirty of those things or more, like some people. But, in the end, it came out really good. It's going to release during the NFR, and I have to say, it's a cute ad. I like doing things that encourage kids to follow their dreams."

She liked that about him. She was sure that he had

completely won the kid over more than he had been a fan before he had met Bret. "I'm sure it will be wonderful."

"So how is your job search going?"

She took a sip of her water. "Honestly, I haven't looked. So far, Mom is so excited about me being here, and I'll tell you, your two sisters-in-law are amazing. We're doing a wedding week after next for a friend of your brother Austin's. He's another physician at the hospital. And it's going to be beautiful. And I don't know…I'm enjoying myself, so I haven't sent out any resumes. Although my ex-boss contacted me and asked me if I'd consider doing an article about rodeo athletes in general. Not about you but about an insider's view of the sport."

"Oh yeah, and what did you say?"

She wasn't sure whether he was wanting her to say she turned it down flat or whether he wouldn't care if she said yes or not. "I told him I'd think about it."

"Really? So is he going to hire you back if you do it?"

"He said there was a possibility but I told him I

wasn't sure about that either. I'm thinking that if I do any journalism articles, it would be in more of a freelance type situation."

"I see. Well, that would give you more freedom to live wherever you wanted to live, wouldn't it?"

Was he hoping she would stay here? "Yes, it would. I wouldn't have to live wherever the job was."

They stared at each other and she was curious whether he just wasn't saying he wanted her to stay here or whether he was just giving her space to decide that on her own. She didn't want to tell him that until she figured out what was going on between them, she wouldn't commit to staying here or leaving. Whether he knew it or not, he was the deciding factor. She knew that she was falling head over heels in love with him again. With just the short time she had been here and renewing their friendship, she knew her feelings had never died. But despite this supposedly being them renewing a friendship and not a romance, she knew that, in the end, if her heart was broken again, she couldn't stay. Of course, she was walking into this with her eyes wide open. She could turn away at any time but like a moth drawn to that proverbial flame, she couldn't look away.

* * *

Bret felt joy as he sat in the booth close to Ellie.

He had wanted to see her all week. And, yes, tomorrow night's ride might be harder because he was going to travel that day and get on the bull, but it wasn't abnormal and he had decided getting back here and just seeing her, even if she didn't want to have dinner with him, would be worth it. Now, looking at her, it was completely worth it. Their conversations had just been about mundane subjects about life in general; they'd laughed at things that had gone on in the world, things that he'd seen during the week or things she'd seen during the week. They had kept things friendly but he had enjoyed hearing her laugh, her voice. And he had hugged her briefly twice when she was in Missouri and he ached to hug her again. He ached to hold her longer. And he had been thinking constantly about kissing her.

"Our family is gearing up for Thanksgiving. I'm guessing the days will have cooled off a little by then. They're already colder after you get out of Texas. What are you and your mom going to do this year? Just the two of you?"

"Yes. It's the second year since Dad died, we've kept it just the two of us. I may see if Mom wants to go for a road trip. Maybe have Thanksgiving in the Ozarks or something."

"That sounds fun. I'm sure if you wanted to, y'all could come out to the ranch and have Thanksgiving with us." He knew throwing that out there may be pushing it a little too much, that she might take it as being or going further than friendship. But maybe not. Just in case, he added, "You know, it is Thanksgiving, and friends and families get together and share Thanksgiving dinner with friends and family."

She toyed with her napkin. "Thanks. I'll mention that to Mom. Your mother may have already mentioned something like that to her—I'm not sure. You know, they talk. Just because your mom is traveling, I think they're in Florida right now, doesn't mean their friendship has wavered any. Those two are like two peas in a pod. As a matter of fact, I know on one of the calls your mom was trying to talk my mom into coming down and visiting them. Wherever they're staying is beautiful and they've made some friends down there. I'm not certain, but I'm a little curious as to whether or not your mom is trying to matchmake a little bit. My dad hasn't been gone all that long but my mother…who knows, she might be getting lonely. I don't know but I'm sure your mother gets more information than I do. I think Mom tries to protect me from her emotions and, you know, things like that. Parents try to protect their kids from how they are truly feeling. So I'm very grateful to your mom."

Unable to help himself, he reached over and laid his hand on hers that was fidgeting with the napkin. Her hand was cool beneath his warm hand. "I hope you know that I'm glad we started this friendship, and I want you to know that if you need anything, I'm here for you. It's kind of crazy how we were so angry all these years and now we're forging this new friendship. And, Ellie, I feel sometimes like all those years have just melted away. And I need you to know that I truly, truly am sorry for any pain that I caused you back then."

Her gaze lifted to his and he saw a shimmer of tears. His mouth went dry and he knew he had touched something deep inside her. "I've been thinking. We were young. Just like you mentioned that day at the river. And when I was out there on the road, I was, in my mind, completely loyal to you. I had my heart set on you. But there were distractions, and it did get lonely, and I did forget that you couldn't see me talking to other gals meant nothing. And then with the tabloids going berserk, it just fueled hurt for you. Even though I can promise you there was nothing brewing between me and any of those people, I was wrong. I should have realized how badly you were being hurt on this end, seeing all those false stories and all those pictures with me and those other gals.

"And, yeah, sometimes I was standing too close to them. I was just dumb and stupid, you know? And, in truth, I'm sure that those gals had other things on their mind. I mean, I'm not stupid. I know that I'm a little bit of a magnet because of all the money we came into when we hit that oil. But I was just a dumb guy. I'm not making excuses. I'm taking full and complete responsibility for everything that happened. Took me long enough to come to that point, didn't it?"

She placed her other hand over his. "Bret, first, you are a female magnet with or without your money. You could be stone-cold broke and still be chased by every woman you came in contact with. And it did hurt. If we're going to be real about it, it did hurt, and I was too young to process that what you were telling me was the truth, that nobody meant anything to you and nothing was going on. I did have a green jealous monster in me, and I had a lot of self-esteem issues going on because of it. But I was wrong in just deciding all of a sudden that I wanted out. I decided on my own that it was easier for me to walk away and go find something else to do that seemed really important and, to be honest, would maybe make you look at me down the road and see this ultra-successful journalist who you had hurt and let go.

"And so I walked away and I lied to you. I told

you I was going to college and that I'd found someone else. I hadn't found anybody else. That guy I dated was just somebody I met and dated a few times. There was nothing serious between us. I never had even kissed him. And when I finally did, he didn't kiss me back. It wasn't his fault—he was a really nice guy. But he knew the whole time I wasn't over you. And I credit him for at least hanging in there. But he knew, too, that night there was nothing there, so we broke it off."

They just stared at each other as their food arrived. And after the waitress left, Bret didn't move; he just looked out around the sparsely filled dining room, his mind processing all that she had said. Guilt rode hard on him—and regret. They had stopped holding hands when the food had been delivered. Now he reached under the table for her hand, which was now in her lap. He pulled it onto the bench between them. "So where does that leave us now? Because, Ellie, I need you to know that my feelings for you are far from just friends. And I don't want to do anything that messes up that friendship but I still have feelings for you. I want to kiss you so bad—but I know we're not there yet."

Ellie looked away then back to him. "I have feelings too but I'm still figuring things out."

Disappointment hoverd over him but at least she was honest. "Then let's eat and visit. I've missed visiting with you."

She smiled. "Good idea."

* * *

Ellie's heart was working overtime after dinner as Bret followed her out to her mother's house to make sure she got home safely and also to say hi to her mom.

When he walked in the back door, Betty looked up from where she was sitting at the breakfast table, with her foot propped up on a chair. "Well, look who is walking in my door! Bret! Young man, come over here and give me a hug."

He walked over, bent down and gave her a hug.

Ellie's heart clenched a little tighter. She was so gone. Just so over-the-top gone where it came to this man.

Her mom patted him on the back.

He stood and pushed his hat back. "So how are you feeling? You about to start getting around better?"

"Oh, I'm doing a lot better. I'm actually walking now, but I'm sitting with my foot up because after being at work all day, it gets kind of tired. But I've been out of the boot for a few days."

"Well, that's good to know. And I hear from my sisters-in-law that this girl here's doing good by you, that she's keeping things rolling."

Her mom beamed up at him. "Ellie's doing amazing, just like I knew she would. She's a natural not only with the flowers but with the people, and her creativity is coming out. You know, as a little girl, she was always creating things. She had a big imagination, and that's one of the things that comes in handy with floral arranging and events. So she's a keeper."

He smiled from Betty to her. "Yes, ma'am. I know what you mean."

Ellie felt a little uncomfortable at that point. She hadn't always been a keeper.

"So you two," she said. "Are y'all going to keep talking about me like I'm not here? Because I am."

They both laughed. Bret grinned at her. "I'm just messing with you, Ellie. Look, Ms. Seton, I just came to say hi and see how you were doing. I flew in tonight to take Ellie to dinner, and I have a couple of things to do with Jake before I leave, but I wanted to come by and see you and make sure you're doing okay."

"I'm doing great. Thank you for coming to check on me. I'm really surprised that you took Ellie out to dinner, but I'm happy about it. I just, well, I want you two to be happy, whatever that takes. I'm just going to say I'm glad to see you two talking after all this time. Your mother is too."

"Yes, ma'am. She already told me that, but I guess me and Ellie just needed time to grow up, maybe. I don't know…I don't want to say anything wrong, but it's a complicated situation, what happened between us. But I'm glad we're on a friendly basis again. Anyway, I've got to go. But if you need anything, you call me. I might be across the country but I'll make sure it happens, whatever you need."

"Oh, get out of here. You know I'm not going to call you, especially if you're across the country. I've got plenty of friends 'round here who can help me out. But thank you very much, young man."

Ellie shook her head as she followed him out of the room, seeing her mother mouth the words *What is going on*. She just shook her head and followed him, closing the door behind her. "I told you that you were going to stir things up if you came in here to say hi to my mom. Now she and your mom are probably going to have us halfway married. When Mom realized that I had flown out to be at that event in Springfield, it was all I could do to tell her that it was just me going out there while we tried to work on our friendship. Now, I don't know…we may be getting their hopes up."

They had reached the truck. He opened the door and had one hand propped at the top of it as he leaned toward her. "Ellie, I thought I made myself clear at dinner that I was wanting to take it further than where we had taken it."

Her cheeks heated. She was in denial and she knew it. "I know. I'm just being cautious."

He stared at her for a long moment and she held his gaze, determined not to look away. And then he reached out with his free arm, snaked it around her back, and gently tugged her toward him. It was an easy, unforced action, giving her plenty of time to step out of the arm that was laid across her lower back. She didn't step aside; she stepped forward so that their bodies were brushing.

With his one arm still holding the top of the door, he leaned his forehead so that it touched hers. "Ellie, I am interested and it's taking everything I have not to kiss you. So I'm just going to come out and ask you. Can I?"

Could he kiss her? She about had a heart attack in the restaurant when he had first mentioned it. But now they were alone, and she knew good and well she was a hypocrite if she said no because she wanted to kiss him too. But she couldn't say anything, so while his forehead was against her forehead, she nodded. She saw him smile, and then his arm tugged her a little closer and his lips covered hers.

It was a slow, gentle, warm kiss, full of emotions. There was so much that happened inside her body with that brief, wonderful touch of his lips to hers. Her arm wrapped around his waist and her hands fisted in the loose cotton of his shirt. He deepened the kiss and her knees weakened. This was what had happened to her every time this man kissed her. Nothing like this had ever filled her with anyone else's kiss. And she knew what the difference was: she loved Bret Tanner. She loved him deeply—sometimes foolishly, but always. She was breathless when he released her.

His eyes were deep with color and sincere as he squinted at her. "I hope I didn't just run you off because, darling, that's the last thing I want to do."

"I'm not running." Then she smiled and a wonderful burst of joy radiated through her entire body. And she prayed that this time would work out.

CHAPTER FIFTEEN

The wedding was beautiful. Ellie stood beside Rita and Tulip as they stood to the side and watched the guests enjoying the beautiful setting of the reception. Ellie's pride at what they accomplished hummed through her. She had loved doing this. Yes, she had enjoyed her job interviewing interesting people, but they were mostly celebrities and she had grown tired of their almost elite vision of themselves. Not all of them, but many of them didn't fully have a grasp on reality. And between that and this—a wedding for a young couple whose parents and friends and family were gathered to wish them a happy life— she knew what was much more of a reward to Ellie. She had helped create the flowers that were used. Yes, this happened to be a wealthy family and the flowers were far more extensive than a wedding on a budget, but Ellie and the girls had done a wedding just as beautiful in a more simple setting with more simple flowers and Ellie had felt just as much pride. Seeing the joy and happiness on everyone's face was an addictive feeling. "Girls, I love this."

Rita nudged her with her elbow. "I knew you would. I told Tulip that I had a feeling you were going to just love doing this. It's a little different than being constantly in the florist shop behind a florist decoration desk. Same with me with photography. I get to get out and I love it."

"Same here," Tulip piped in with a chuckle. "I'm an outdoorsy type girl, anyway, so if I had to be stuck indoors all the time, I would go crazy. My Cole would have to spend all his money taking me on trips so I wouldn't go crazy all the time."

They all laughed at that.

Ellie knew all the Tanner brothers. And they were—and had been from early on—regular guys, young cowboys who loved the land and loved riding horses and working cattle and playing in a river. The vision of Bret in low-riding swim trunks, teenage muscles bulging as he clung to a rope and swung out over the river and then cannonballed into the cool water, filled her mind. "I guess I've known Bret and his brothers longer than any of y'all, and they've always been just laid-back, regular guys. I remember when their family struck oil. It was life-changing. Bret and I had been dating and he and his brothers all seem to handle it in different ways. Well, you know, at first, there was that initial excitement of suddenly being wealthier than you could have ever imagined. That was quickly replaced with the total realization that their lives had just changed. Bret never faltered, though, on his dream of becoming a NFR champion. He didn't have to go get his body banged up on the back of a bull in order to make a living any longer, and yet that was his dream and he did it anyway. I think Levi and Jake struggled with handling it because they were younger and I'm so glad to see them both mature and handling it in such great ways. Cole and Austin—those two were always steady as a rock."

"Levi said that he and Jake struggled, but he got over that. And I can tell you he is not a fan of the paparazzi. And I don't think any of them are. Bret's kind of more adjusted to it than any of them because of what he does. But thankfully, through the years, they've adjusted and are well rounded. That benefit that they held for cancer research for the cancer wing at the hospital was such a blessing and such a good way to use the platform of wealth that they have been given."

Tulip nodded in agreement with what Rita said. "Cole loved doing that. And he's told me that up until recently, he had been thinking about doing more but he's loving being more settled now and starting a foundation with his brothers to do more things like that. And luckily, with the three of us and our partnership, we have exactly the support that they need for putting things like that together. That thrills me. And I'm loving the landscaping part of it. I was thrilled to be a part of getting this garden ready for such an occasion."

Satisfaction filled Ellie and she knew that this

partnership was meant to be. It was still startling to her how she was brought back here, through the loss of a job and the accident of her mom and, most oddly of all, to try to get an interview from Bret. She pushed down the sudden, almost painful knot that formed in her chest thinking about the family she still wanted to have, the family that belonged to her and Bret. Hope radiated through her and deep, heartfelt wishes were like bubbles lifting into the air. Prayers that all of her long-ago hopes and dreams could possibly be coming true.

Bret's kiss before he had left yesterday had done that for her. She prayed that right now he was having a good ride because she knew that it was nearing time for him to be on the back of that bull. He had been excited when he left. And yet he had been sad. He told her that he was finding it harder and harder to be away while knowing that she was here in town. His words had been a balm to her aching heart and had given way to more hope that their relationship could fully be healed.

The bride and groom took the mic from the band

leader and, arm in arm, they pointed to Ellie, Rita, and Tulip. "Me and my bride," the grinning groom said, "wanted to give a shout-out to three of the most amazing wedding planning women—I guess we'd say wedding planning team. You ladies have done a remarkable job and this wedding has been everything that my bride wished it to be. And, on my behalf, I thank you for that. All I could do was show up and hope that I was enough, but with you three at the helm, you rode it on in and brought it home. Thank you from the bottom of our hearts. And if any of you out there are thinking about getting married or holding a benefit or anything, we can completely give this group, our whole-hearted recommendation."

Everyone joined in clapping and Ellie, along with her two partners, gave a small bow of their heads and then lifted their hands and waved in thank-you.

* * *

"You're crazy," Jake drawled, his voice completely full of disbelief.

"Yeah, I know, man. I knew you'd say that. I kind

of feel crazy but I can't help myself. I'm fixing to touch down in thirty minutes and I need you to come pick me up." It was three a.m. and Bret was on a private jet, headed toward True Love. Actually, headed toward Stonewall to the McCoy private airport. He needed his brother to crawl out of bed and come pick him up. He knew Jake would but not before he trashed him with how stupid he was being.

"Well, I'm already getting up because I know as crazy as you are, if I called you at three in the morning and drug you out of bed, you'd be there for me. And I've got to tell ya, I'm glad you and Ellie are working things out. It just feels right. She know you're coming back into town?"

"No. She'd probably tell me I'm crazy, too, but I've got to see her. I can't help it."

Jake laughed. "Well, I'll be heading out in a minute. I'll be at the airport waiting for you."

"I figured you would. You're a good man, Jake Tanner."

He was smiling as he hung the phone up and leaned back into the plush leather of the seats of the private jet. He was spending money like it was made of water, and he didn't really care. He'd never asked for this oil money that boiled up out of their land like it was a flowing river. But now he was glad to use it. It helped him be able to come home and see his sweetheart. He grinned at the thought. Yeah, he had it bad and he knew it.

He closed his eyes, ignoring his aching shoulder. He had barely eked out a win tonight. His standings were solid; he was still the one to beat at the NFR in Las Vegas this year. But he didn't even really care. Right now, the thing at the top of the leaderboard for him was Ellie. And he knew she always would be. There wasn't anything in this world that would ever get between him and his love for her again.

* * *

Ellie woke to the soft tapping sound on her window. She looked at the clock; it was 3:45 a.m. She listened. A chill rang through her as she realized the tapping noise on her window was intentional. *Who would be tapping on her window at this early hour?* At first, she was tempted to not even go over and pull back her curtains, afraid of what she might see. But she lived at her mama's place, out in the country; there was nobody out here tapping on her window who was going to do her harm. Her heart gave a little ker-thunk. *Could it be Bret?* Surely not. Of anybody she could think of who might be tapping on her window, he was the only one. But he was in Cheyenne, Wyoming.

She crawled out of bed, eased over to the window, and gently cracked the curtain just enough. Then she heard it.

"Open the window, Ellie. It's me, Bret."

She couldn't hardly see him because of the dim light, but she could make out a form and her heart began to jump erratically in her chest. She pulled back the curtain, undid the latches, and lifted the window. He stood in the flower bed, grinning at her. He had on a felt cowboy hat, a gray T-shirt, jeans and boots. His hair was tussled and he looked tired as heck but oh, did he look good.

"What are you doing here?"

"Well, I thought it was obvious. I'm here to see you."

"But it's almost four a.m. Aren't you supposed to be in Cheyenne?"

"Well, I was there and I won at bull riding, but then I got on an airplane and here I am. I would've been here sooner but the bull riders were thick as thieves tonight. I had to wait until all of them got through before I could head this way."

She was grinning from ear to ear. "I can't believe it, but I am so glad to see you. And I'm glad you won."

He cupped her face through the open window and tugged her toward him as he stepped close, with the windowsill between them. He cocked his head to the side and kissed her lips while his thumbs traced the lines of her jaw. She sighed into his mouth, loving the feel of him, loving that he had flown all the way home after a strenuous bull ride just to be with her.

"I can't get you off my mind, Ellie. I think about you constantly. I almost didn't even ride tonight. I couldn't help it...I almost called and got that plane earlier and came home then."

"I miss you, too, and I'm really glad you're missing me. But you've got to ride—you know you're going to ride."

"I don't know any such thing. I've got to tell you, Ellie, this isn't like before, when I was a young, snot-nosed kid with a dream of being the leader champion in bull riding and forgetting what was important in my real life, not my professional life. Right now, nothing matters to me but you. Nothing."

"Wow. You've got to stay focused, Bret. I know you're saying that but I know you don't mean that. Riding bulls means everything to you and you're favored to win this year, so you need to get your mind off me and start focusing on riding."

He grinned, kissed her lips very quickly, and pulled back, laughing. "Ellie Seton…worrying about whether I'm going to win the NFR. Back it up, buttercup. I couldn't care less whether I win or lose this year. What's important is you."

He kissed her and she melted into him as the windowsill made it awkward for both of them.

"So now what?" she asked.

"Well, it's four a.m. I was too restless and anxious to sleep on the plane, and my shoulder is pretty stressed out and throbbing pretty good, so now that I got my kiss and I got to see you, I guess I'll drive back home and lay down for a few hours."

"What if—since I'm now up and probably not going to sleep for a while—what if you came in and I made myself a pot of coffee and you go lay down in the guest room, and then I'll wake you up in a couple of hours?"

"You sure?"

"Yes, I'm sure. Come on. I'll go open the back door for you. Meet you there."

She closed the window as he stepped back and started walking toward the corner where he would turn and go to the back door. She grabbed a robe and pulled it over her T-shirt and sleep shorts. She was still grinning when she walked into the kitchen and to the door to unlock it.

He came inside and immediately swept her into his arms, holding her close and breathing her in. He kissed her ear, kissed her jaw, and then kissed her lips again. "I didn't dream you were going to ask me to come in and sleep on the bed back there, but I'm going to do it because that means as soon as I wake up, I get to see you again."

She laughed, feeling so happy inside. "Well, don't you know the reason I asked you to do that was so that when you woke up, I get to see you?"

He cupped her jaw between his hands. "Am I reading things wrong, or have we crossed the line into forbidden territory?"

She knew what he was asking. She knew he was asking whether they were on their way to falling in love, the forbidden territory of a place they weren't sure they wanted to go. "I think you're right. I think that once we started down that path, our emotions were woken up and just started rolling like a snowball, gathering steam all the way down a snow-covered mountain."

He grinned and it tickled her all the way through. "I like that analogy. Right now, I'm rolling pretty fast. I'm crazy about you. And I just want you to know that like I said before—or did I say it before? I let my hopes and dreams and my immaturity cloud my vision before, but now I've got you in my high beams, girl, and there ain't nothing that means more to me than you."

With that, he turned and walked down the hallway. He knew where the guest room was; he had been to her mom's house before. Though he had never slept in that room, the door was always open and the house wasn't that big. She watched him as he paused at the door before he went inside. He grinned at her. She smiled at him, and then he went inside and closed the door.

With a sigh, she turned and went to the coffeemaker. She needed a really strong cup of coffee. 'Cause she was in so much trouble. She was in love, and if what he just said was true, he was too. Was it too much to hope for?

CHAPTER SIXTEEN

Bret strode into the kitchen about seven-thirty. The rich scent of coffee pulled him over to the coffeemaker, where he poured himself a hot cup. He turned and leaned against the kitchen counter and raked a hand through his tousled hair. His body hurt but he smiled as he realized he was standing in Ellie's mom's kitchen. There was a note on the counter, he saw, and picked it up. "In the shower. Will be right out. Enjoy a cup of coffee. Warm biscuits and sausage in the oven."

He smiled, set it down, took a drink of his coffee, letting the warmth seep into him and his foggy brain. *How would it feel to not have to feel this beat up every morning? To roll over in bed and find Ellie there cuddled next to him?* The thought warmed him and made him wish for things he better not think about right now. He heard a door open and a moment later, he anticipated Ellie walking in. Instead, it was her mom.

Betty smiled at him. "Well, good morning. And how are you, world traveler? Ellie told me you had surprised her with a few tappings on her window this morning. Did you sleep okay?"

"Yes, ma'am, I did. I hope you don't mind me showing up like that. I finished up my rodeo last night and I just couldn't stay away." He looked at the older woman and saw a bit of wariness in her eyes. "Ms. Betty, I know that I hurt your daughter back when we were dating and I rode off into the sunset—pretty much abandoned her. I didn't really even mean to. I was just young and stupid, I guess. I didn't even know I was doing it but on reflection, yeah, I know I did that and I'm trying to repair my past mistakes. And I don't know if Ellie's going to have me, but I just want to thank you for not having—or at least it doesn't seem like you've held—a grudge against me. I know my mom has said that you and her had hopes, but y'all didn't really discuss it all that much."

Betty walked over and patted his arm as she reached for the coffee pot. "Bret, your mom and I realize that what was going on between you and Ellie was between you and Ellie, and that our friendship couldn't be based on what the two of you did. And we also both felt like if it was meant to be, it would have been. You were young and you had stars in your eyes. You had a lot going on with the oil strike and the paparazzi and the fame that you gathered up suddenly. I'm not excusing what you did, but I can understand it. My Ellie, she's strong and she's an overcomer. And you can see she has. So I'm just going to leave it at this: What's between you and Ellie is still between you and Ellie. You both have my heartfelt encouragement but I will say that if you've flown all the way back into her life like this and are stirring up or renewing emotions in her, only to just fly away again, then my feelings won't be as easy this time for you. You aren't doing that, are you?"

"No, ma'am. I'm not doing that. I wouldn't have

come back if I hadn't realized that I want Ellie in my life. And I told her that last night, but she hasn't said anything. I've been thinking about it and people may think I'm crazy, but if Ellie would have me, I'd walk away from bull riding right now."

Betty stepped back and studied him. Her expression was quizzical. "I think you're serious about that. And why would you do that now? You're sitting at the top of the leaderboard—you're the favored one this year."

"I've been there before and that buckle and all that fame or recognition—I wouldn't call it fame like a movie star or anything like that—I'm realizing, when I got off that bull last night and everyone was clapping me on the shoulder because it was a good ride, I was limping and my shoulder was hurting, and all I could think about was getting back here and seeing Ellie. None of that gave me any comfort. I got up this morning in a bed all by my lonesome like I normally am but at least there was the comfort that Ellie was down the hall from me. And in a minute, she's going to walk through that door and I hope she's going to walk into my arms. I realize last night that's what I want…that's what I need, and I'm asking if that's okay with you?"

"If what's okay with her?" Ellie asked from the doorway.

Betty patted his arm. "Yes." Then she smiled, took her coffee, and walked back down the hallway and closed the door behind her.

Ellie smiled at him. "I don't know what you and Mom were talking about but she gave me a little smile before she walked by. Y'all must have had a good talk. I have to say, I like seeing you in the kitchen in the morning."

The light in her eyes had him setting his coffee down and he held his arms open. To his utter happiness, she strode across the room and into his arms. He wrapped them around her, felt her body mold into his body. His heart rammed into his chest so hard he thought it would come out. *This. This was what he wanted.* He kissed her temple and then he lifted her chin and looked into her big, beautiful eyes.

"I think that you and I have some talking to do.

You up for taking a little ride?"

"Sure. But don't you have to catch a plane and fly off to a rodeo somewhere?"

"Not today, darling. Come on."

He took her hand, wanting to kiss her. But he didn't; he led her out through the back door and opened the ranch truck he was driving. He opened the passenger door and waited until she got in. Then he grinned at her, leaned in and kissed her lips. Closing the door, he strode around the front to the driver's seat and climbed in. "Buckle up, buttercup. Here we go."

She laughed and they just grinned at each other. Happiness throbbed through him and he knew this was right. He drove down the country road. It wound through the scrub brush and rambling oak trees and desperado sage that bloomed with its purple flowers and dusty green leaves along the way. When he reached the parking area that he had been driving to, he parked the truck and went around and met her on the passenger side.

He took her hand and strode down the little path that led down to their spot on the river. They walked quietly down the path together. How many times had they made this trip? The last time they made this trip, they hadn't been together and it hadn't ended well. He hated to say thank goodness her mother fell off that ladder and hurt her ankle, but some things happen in crazy ways and good had come from that accident. Ellie had stayed in town and had to come around him, and he'd had to put up with her around him. If it hadn't been for that benefit, he had been such a hothead and so angry he probably would have called a plane out of there and not stuck around. Thank God, that hadn't been the plan.

When they reached the bottom of the ravine, he led her over to the rock and then he took both of her hands. They stood there, looking at each other. A smile twitched at the edge of her lips and her expression was one of questioning. But she didn't say anything and he knew she was just holding out for him to speak his mind.

He squeezed her hands. "Ellie, I'm announcing my retirement tomorrow."

Her expression was of shock. "But why? Are you okay? Have you been hurt more?"

He smiled. And then he laughed. "No, I haven't been hurt. I've taken a good hard look at everything and now I'm taking a good hard look at you. And I'll tell you this, like I told your mom this morning: when I got off that bull last night, it was a great ride—one of the best in my career. But that ride's not going to keep me warm at night or give me joy in the day. I win them and then I set them aside. They're a dime a dozen—well, not really but you know what I mean. But you are a jewel. You are once in a lifetime and I don't want to lose you. I want you in my life for the rest of my life, and I don't want to be so beat up and banged up or crippled or mangled or hurting every morning. I want to enjoy my life with you, so I'm retiring." Hanging onto her hands, he went down to one knee.

She gasped. "What are you doing?"

He grinned. "I'm doing what I should have done a long, long time ago. Ellie Seton, I'm asking you from the bottom of my heart, will you be my wife? Will you let me love you and spend the rest of my life with you and give you everything I have, but mostly my heart and my love?"

Tears trickled down her cheeks. "I will. But you don't have to retire."

He stood up, wrapped her in his arms, and kissed her. "Oh yes, I do, darling, because I don't want to spend another night on the road. I want to spend them here in True Love, in our house, on our own piece of property, raising our own set of kids. Those little kids have been haunting my days for years and I think it's about time we get started bringing them into this world."

She laughed against his lips. "I think that you, Bret Tanner, have the best idea in the world."

Also from Hope Moore

Thank you for reading! Want to be the first to know about exclusive promotions, news, giveaways and new releases? Sign up for my newsletter here: www.subscribepage.com/hopemooresignup

Reviews help other readers find new books. I always appreciate when my readers take time to leave and honest review. It is so helpful to me!

I love hearing from my readers. Please feel free to contact me at authorhopemoore@gmail.com

About the Author

Hope Moore is the pen name of an award-winning author who lives deep in the heart of Texas surrounded by Christian cowboys who give her inspiration for all of her inspirational sweet romances. She loves writing clean & wholesome, swoon worthy romances for all of her fans to enjoy and share with everyone. Her heartwarming, feel good romances are full of humor and heart, and gorgeous cowboys and heroes to love. And the spunky women they fall in love with and live happily-ever-after.

When she isn't writing, she's trying very hard not to cook, since she could live on peanut butter sandwiches, shredded wheat, coffee...and cheesecake why should she cook? She loves writing though and creating new stories is her passion. Though she does love shoes, she's admitted she has an addiction and tries really hard to stay out of shoe stores. She, however, is not addicted to social media and chooses to write instead of surf FB - but she LOVES her readers so she's working on a free novella just for you and if you sign up for her newsletter she will send it to you as soon as its ready! You'll also receive snippets of her adventures, along with special deals, sneak peaks of soon-to-be released books and of course any sales she might be having.

She promises she will not spam you, she hates to be spammed also, so she wouldn't dare do that to people she's crazy about (that means YOU). You can unsubscribe at any time.

Sign up for my newsletter:
www.subscribepage.com/hopemooresignup

I can't wait to hear from you.

Hope Moore~
Always hoping for more love, laughter and reading for you every day of your life!

www.ingramcontent.com/pod-product-compliance
Lightning Source LLC
Chambersburg PA
CBHW070641100726

47907CB00007B/2058